Aunt Safiyya and the Monast

LITERATURE OF THE MIDDLE EAST

a series of fiction, poetry, and memoirs in translation

TITLES PUBLISHED AND IN PRESS

Memoirs from the Women's Prison, by Nawal El Saadawi
translated by Marilyn Booth

Arabic Short Stories
translated by Denys Johnson-Davies

The Innocence of the Devil, by Nawal El Saadawi
translated by Sherif Hetata

Memory for Forgetfulness: August, Beirut, 1982
by Mahmoud Darwish
translated by Ibrahim Muhawi

Aunt Safiyya and the Monastery, by Bahaa' Taher
translated by Barbara Romaine

Aunt Safiyya and the Monastery

A Novel

Bahaa' Taher

Translated from the Arabic by Barbara Romaine

UNIVERSITY OF CALIFORNIA PRESS

Berkeley Los Angeles London

This book is published with the support of a grant from
the Reves Center for International Studies
at the College of William and Mary.

University of California Press
Berkeley and Los Angeles, California

University of California Press, Ltd.
London, England

Library of Congress Cataloging-in-Publication Data

Ṭāhir, Bahā', 1935–
[Khālatī Ṣafīyah wa-al-dayr. English]
Aunt Safiyya and the monastery : a novel / Bahaa' Taher ; translated from the Arabic by Barbara Romaine.
p. cm. — (Literature of the Middle East)
ISBN 0-520-20074-8 (alk. paper). — ISBN 0-520-20075-6 (pbk. : alk. paper)
I. Romaine, Barbara, 1959– . II. Title. III. Series.
PJ7864.A357K4613 1996
892'.736—dc20 95-38100
CIP

Printed in the United States of America
9 8 7 6 5 4 3 2

The paper used in this publication meets the minimum requirements of American National Standard for Information Sciences—Permanence of Paper for Printed Library Materials, ANSI Z39.48-1984.

To my daughters,
Dina and Yusr,
with love to them
and to my country

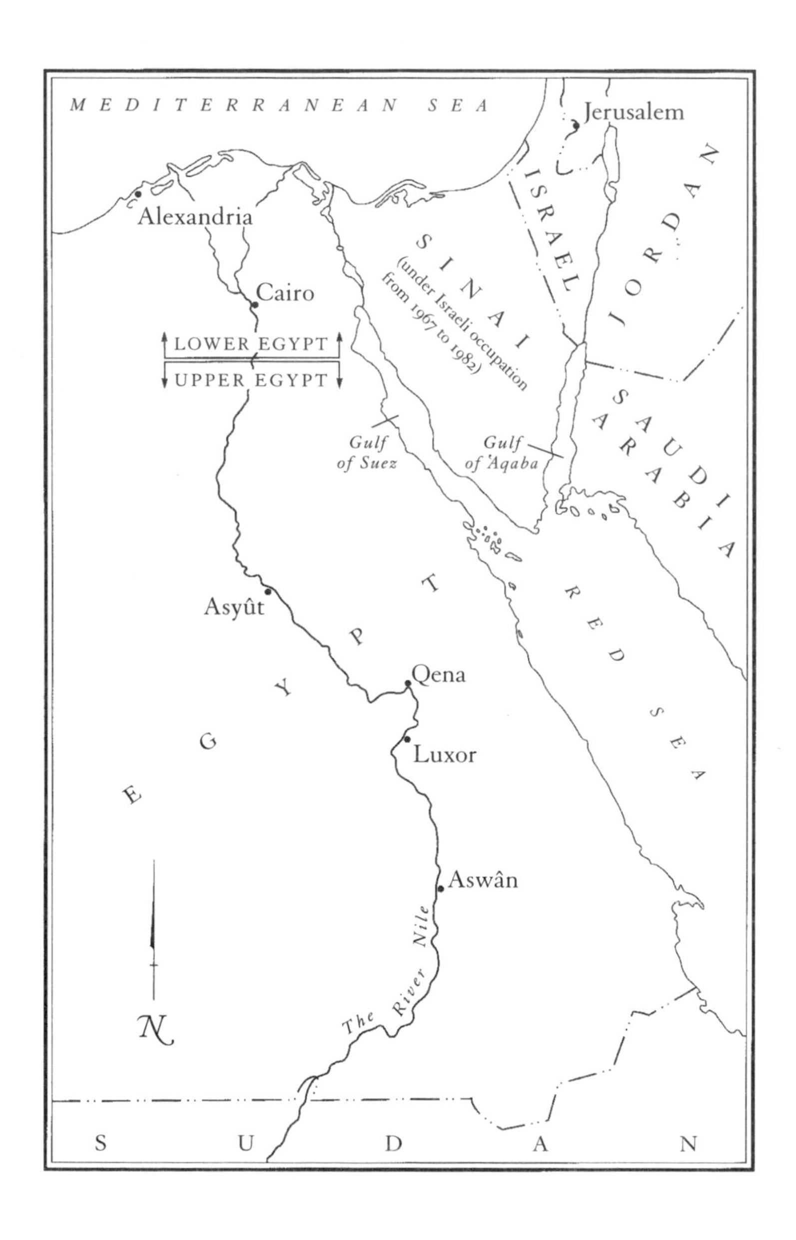

MEDITERRANEAN SEA
Jerusalem
Alexandria
ISRAEL
JORDAN
SINAI
(under Israeli occupation from 1967 to 1982)
Cairo
LOWER EGYPT
UPPER EGYPT
SAUDI ARABIA
Gulf of Suez
Gulf of 'Aqaba
Asyût
EGYPT
RED SEA
Qena
Luxor
Aswân
The River Nile
N
SUDAN

CONTENTS

ACKNOWLEDGMENTS

This translation would never have been possible without the assistance, both spiritual and material, of innumerable friends, colleagues, and relatives, some of whom must unfortunately go unnamed here, in the interest of keeping my acknowledgments to a length somewhat less than that of the novel itself!

I must begin by thanking the author of the original work, Bahaaʾ Taher, first of all for allowing me the opportunity of translating his beautiful novel, my admiration for which provided the spark of inspiration for the translation; I must thank Mr. Taher as well for his endless, patient assistance on the translation itself, in which he has been a full participant, usually over inconveniently long distances.

Second, I wish to express my utmost appreciation to Lynne Withey of the University of California Press, for encouraging me to publish this novel and then putting up with thousands of E-mail messages from me as a result of her encouragement. She has been unfailingly cheerful and supportive in the face of my unremitting queries and complaints.

Dr. James Bill, director of the Reves Center for International Studies at the College of William and Mary in Williamsburg, Virginia, came through with both financial and moral support at a very crucial juncture. I am profoundly grateful to him and the Reves Center for helping me keep this project on track.

Additional thanks for consultation on the translation itself go to Mr. Taher's friend and colleague, Shafiq Magar, who read the entire manuscript and made detailed comments; to Mohammed Sawaie, who also patiently endured my interminable questions conveyed by E-mail and whose responses were invaluable; to Kristen Brustad, who, going over sections of the translation on which I was stuck, gave me many hours she could scarcely spare; and to John Williams, John Eisele, and many other colleagues more learned than I am who provided both help and encouragement along the way.

To David Wilmsen and Ray Langsten—without whom I might never have had the heart to pursue this project when in its early stages the obstacles seemed insurmountable—many thanks. I thank David in particular for his efforts to help me locate a publisher for the novel.

Elizabeth Oram, who first put me in the way of contacting Bahaa' Taher, and who has been cheering me on ever since, deserves special mention.

I am grateful to my mother, Susan Romaine, my sister, Janet Romaine, and my friend Philip Zimmerman, who read early drafts of the translation with good grace and helpful comments; for advice on the introduction, thanks to my father, William

Romaine, and to friends Carolyn Makinson and Dan Byman, among others.

The following people provided moral support, inspiration, and the answers to many questions: Kassem Shafei, his wife Sahar Gaber, and their daughter Radwa; Dalia Abu-Hagar; Samira Khalil; Nadia Harb; Nabila Assiouti; Hanaaʾ Kilani; Ayman El-Desouki; and Wafaaʾ El-Tayyeb.

Susan Barile, along with her friendship and her belief in me, supplied books that were helpful in researching background material.

Finally, to all those not named here whose good will and encouragement nevertheless made a difference in helping this translation come into being, my sincere gratitude.

To all who have helped bring this project to fruition, heartfelt thanks.

This translation is dedicated to the memory of my mother,
who died in April 1995.

NOTE ON TRANSLITERATION AND PRONUNCIATION

Like all languages, Arabic is full of idioms and words for which there is no exact equivalent in any other language. For the most part, I have tried to get around this with at least an approximate translation, but in a few cases I have found any English rendering of the Arabic to be so awkward as to interfere with the flow of the narrative. In such instances, I have transliterated an Arabic word or expression, explaining it either with a footnote or in the glossary. In general, Arabic words in this text have been transliterated so as to make them, insofar as possible, phonetically intelligible to the non-Arabic speaker. In some cases, phonemes that do not exist in English have been omitted entirely or replaced with similar English phonemes where the presence or absence of the Arabic phoneme—although significant to an Arabic speaker—makes little difference to most English speakers.

A few points call for explanation. In the word *miqaddis* (referring to a Christian pilgrim; see glossary), the *q,* standing for Arabic letter qāf, would in Modern Standard Arabic be pronounced as a velar *k*—that is, in the back of the throat: a sound not present in English. In the narrative, this form of the word is used. In the dialogue, however, the reader will often find the word spelled *migaddis,* following a variation also used in the original Arabic text. In the dialect of Upper Egypt (Saʿiidi Arabic, as opposed to Cairene), the qāf is generally pronounced as a hard *g*. This same phonetic variation will be found with the words *qallayaat/gallayaat* (here referring to monastic "cells") and *qabr/gabr* ("grave"). In words that contain a single open quote, such as *miʿallim* ("boss") and *ʿEid* (Islamic holiday; see glossary), this symbol stands for an Arabic sound for which English has no symbol: that of the letter ʿayn, which represents a phoneme not found in English (almost like the French retroflex *r,* but with no contact between the upper and lower palates as the sound is produced. Similarly, in the word *maʾdhoun* (Islamic official; see glossary), the apostrophe represents the glottal stop heard at the beginning and in the middle of the expression, "uh-oh." The word *shaaʾ* (as in the expression *bismillaahi maa shaaʾ allah;* see glossary) also contains this glottal stop.

GLOSSARY

ʿamm literally "uncle" but used more generally as a title of respect when addressing an elder.

Amosis founder of the eighteenth Dynasty of Egypt: in 1567 B.C., he drove out a group of invaders known as the Hyksos, who had come from the east and ruled Egypt since 1674 B.C.

ʿaraq strong alcoholic drink, distilled from dates.

bekawiya literally, "the rank of a bey."

bismillaahi maa shaaʾ allah "in the name of God, this is what God has willed": Arabs have traditionally feared that beauty may attract the envy of others and therefore bad luck (hence, "the evil eye"); any direct acknowledgment of a person's beauty is thus considered dangerous, so instead the name of God is invoked, as in the expression used here, which is intended to warn the envious that it is wrong to direct envy at God's handiwork.

bey a title of prestigious social rank, at one time awarded by the ruler of Egypt and achieved either by merit or through bribes; it may also be used loosely, simply to address someone in a respectful manner.

Cromer (Lord) the most powerful British administrator (1882–1906) during the British occupation of Egypt.

diwan an area, like a sitting room, either within or at the front part of a house, for receiving guests, usually used by the men of the household and their male visitors.

ʿEid here ʿEid el-Fitr, a major Islamic holiday celebrating the end of Ramadan (q.v.).

el-Baida, el-Halabiyya epithets of Amuna (see p. 37): *el-Baida* means "the white," or "the fair skinned"; *el-Halabiyya*—"the girl from Aleppo"—is not actually part of Amuna's name but refers to a migration from Aleppo, in Syria, to Egypt of a particular group of people who came to be known as gypsies, thus identifying her as a gypsy.

el-Hasan and *el-Hussein* grandsons of the Prophet Muhammad: el-Hussein was murdered in a dispute over the succession to the caliphate, in a battle in Karbala, Iraq; accounts of the death of el-Hasan do not agree, but one variant suggests that he was poisoned.

el-Nigashi the Negus: title of the Christian ruler of Ethiopia in the time of the Prophet Muhammad.

Faris name meaning "horseman" or "cavalier."

feddan measure equivalent to slightly more than an acre.

gallabiyya long robelike garment, traditionally worn by Egyptian peasant men; in winter, other clothes might be worn underneath, including a pair of long underpants.

ghurayyiba sweet biscuits, something like shortbread, traditionally prepared on certain holidays.

gouza also known as *hookah* or *shisha,* a flexible or bamboo pipe attached to a bottlelike container full of water topped by a bowl of burning coals, sometimes used by men for smoking hashish—hence the reference to the "innocent" women's *gouza* (see p. 67).

hagg a term of respect, generally but not invariably referring to a Muslim who has made the pilgrimage to Mecca.

Harbi name meaning "warrior."

Hijra the flight from Mecca to Medina, in A.D. 620, by the Prophet Muhammad and his followers, who were escaping the persecution that was inflicted upon the earliest Muslims.

hookah see *gouza.*

Hyksos see *Amosis.*

imam Muslim prayer leader.

in shaa' allah God willing.

jilbaab long garment similar to a *gallabiyya* (q.v.).

jubbah cloak, or long outer garment, open in front, with wide sleeves.

karkadeh a sweet drink made from hibiscus flowers.

khawaaga Egyptian slang for "foreigner," roughly equivalent to the South American word *gringo.*

maʾdhoun in Islam, an official authorized to perform marriages: the part of the wedding performed by the *maʾdhoun* would traditionally take place in the presence of the groom and some of the wedding guests, before the arrival of the bride.

miʿallim a title of respect, roughly translatable as "master" or "boss."

miqaddis a title normally referring to a Christian who has made the pilgrimage to *Al-Quds* (Jerusalem).

misbaha a string of prayer beads, something like a rosary.

mizmar a single-reed instrument that sounds something like an oboe.

naksa literally, "setback"; sometimes used euphemistically—as in this novel—in reference to the defeat in the 1967 war when Egypt, under Nasser (q.v.), lost Sinai to Israel.

Nasser Gamal Abdel-Nasser, leader of the Egyptian Revolution in 1952 and president of Egypt from 1954 until his death in 1970.

qallayaat literally, "fryers"; actually "cells" (here monastic cells).

Ramadan ninth month in the Islamic calendar; Ramadan is observed in part through daily fasting from dawn to sunset, and the final breaking of the fast, held on the first day of the tenth month (*Shawwaal*), normally involves a great celebration—see also *ʿEid.*

Saʿiid Upper Egypt, known as "the *Saʿiid*"; *Saʿiidi* is the corresponding adjective.

sharbat a sweet drink made from fruit syrup.

shisha see *gouza.*

tarbush the cylindrical "fez," Turkish in origin, usually red with a black tassel.

wallahi literally, "by God," but often used to emphasize whatever is being said or to confirm a previous statement.

Ward es-Sham name meaning "flower of Damascus."

ya vocative particle, generally used in direct address, as in "ya Safiyya!"

INTRODUCTION

Born in Cairo in 1935, Bahaa' Taher began publishing fiction in 1964. He has to his credit several collections of short stories and three novels, of which *Aunt Safiyya and the Monastery,* published in Egypt in 1991, is the third. Raised and educated in the city of his birth, Taher nevertheless feels a strong connection with the geographical setting of this novel: the region of Luxor, where his parents came from. In his introduction to the original work, the author pays tribute to his mother, a gifted storyteller whom he credits with inspiring his own narrative talents. Taher himself is both a first-rate storyteller and a shrewd observer of the world in which he lives, revealing through his fiction a great deal about a broad range of Egyptian experience: from the struggle of daily life in Cairo to the difficulties facing an Egyptian emigrant in Europe to a conflict of ethics and tradition in an Upper Egyptian village.

Taher began his literary career in the wake of the revolution of 1952, which overthrew the monarchy and led to Gamal

Abdel-Nasser's rise to power in 1954, when Taher was a student at Cairo University. In his introduction to *Aunt Safiyya*'s Arabic original, he describes the political demonstrations, in which he participated, against the monarchy and its corrupt administration. He writes of the elation he and his classmates felt at the success of the revolution, as well as their subsequent rapid disillusionment with the new regime.

This was evidently a painfully confusing time for those who had actively supported the revolution and believed in the ideals it represented, which were essentially socialist in character. On the one hand, Taher and his colleagues continued wholeheartedly to believe in the revolution and what it stood for in principle, as long as the struggle was directed toward such goals as restoring Egypt's self-reliance through the rejection of Western interference in the country's affairs—particularly Britain's paternalistic control, which had flourished under the monarchy. On the other hand, if those who had supported the revolution hoped for a strong voice in the new administration, they were largely disappointed, for Nasser's accession to the presidency of Egypt was soon followed by severe crackdowns on individuals and groups that were perceived as in any way threatening to the regime. Thus a period of social reform and a striving for political autonomy in Egypt was also one of political purges and radio broadcasts of the trials of alleged subversives. In his introduction, Taher refers eloquently to the contradictory feelings of loyalty and horror this situation evoked in him and his contemporaries. It was in this atmosphere, he tells us, that he and many others began their literary careers, without fully understanding at the time why they were so confused. Only later, he says, did they gain a more useful perspective on their conflicting feelings.

Many of Taher's earlier stories, written in the 1960s, express the anguish and frustration that came out of that period. A number of them feature characters whose hopes for a prosperous future are dashed in one way or another, or who endure some senseless setback. The characters seem to be more or less paralyzed, as all attempts to reverse their fate have met with defeat; the result is a sense of resigned despair. The reader might read their plight as analogous to the hopes and disappointments the Egyptian people felt in connection with the revolution of 1952.

In Egypt social criticism, ranging from the gently allusive to the scathingly satirical, often finds expression in fiction. A number of Egyptian writers, such as Yusuf Idris and Naguib Mahfouz—who are among the Egyptian authors best known outside the Arab world—have at various times suffered censorship, or worse, as a result of expressing their views too freely. Taher himself, in the mid-1970s (during the administration of Anwar Sadat), was dismissed from his job in radio broadcasting and prevented from publishing his writing. He tells us in his introduction that in his fiction he had generally avoided direct criticism of the political system, but the climate of the times was such that the smallest suggestion of realism in an author's work, implying a less than rosy picture of life in contemporary Egypt, was enough to attract the attention of critics who worked for what Taher calls "the establishment." Using methods chillingly reminiscent of our own McCarthy era, such critics would target these writers and publicly denounce them as Communists, among other things. Having thus come under the critics' fire and been deprived of the opportunity to work, Taher was eventually obliged to leave his beloved Egypt to seek a livelihood elsewhere; in 1981 he moved to Geneva. There he found a position as a translator for the United Nations, where he is employed to this day, although he continues to regard writing as his most important occupation.

Bahaa' Taher is a storyteller first and a social commentator second. The commentary underlying his clear and direct prose is certainly integral to his stories, but the language is kept deliberately simple, with a strong emphasis on descriptive detail, punctuated by action depicted in straightforward narrative style. There is plenty of scope for analysis, but such probing is left mainly to the reader, for the narrator of the story is generally himself a participant in the events and thus expresses a limited, not omniscient, viewpoint.

The simplicity and directness of Taher's prose do not, however, preclude a delicate ambiguity. This is expressed in the characterization of the people who come to life in his novels and short stories, for they cannot be said to stand unequivocally for such qualities as innocence, honesty, corruption, ambition, guile, and so forth. Neither Taher's characters nor the narrative context in which they exist can be pinned down to a system of values in which right and wrong, good and bad, or true and false are defined in absolute terms. In other words, Taher poses questions, setting out certain problems in high relief for the reader's consideration, but—although he has an unmistakable purpose in mind—he does not serve up tidy resolutions or sweeping conclusions.

For example, consider "In an Unusual Park," a short story depicting a chance meeting between an Egyptian expatriate and a native of the unnamed European country in which the Egyptian has settled. The story begins when the protagonist accidentally wanders into a park that has been specially created for people to walk their dogs. On realizing where he is, he reacts first with dismay, then with rage as he thinks how many starving Egyptian children could be fed on what these Europeans feed their dogs. Before he can get away, however, he is drawn unwillingly into a conversation with an elderly woman, who is walking her dog in the park. He tries repeatedly to extricate himself from this conversation, in the course of which the woman soon reveals her own naïveté about foreigners in general and Egyptians in particular. Yet she is fully as sympathetic a character as the protagonist himself, even though she and her dog represent the culture in which he feels so alienated. As the old woman's story unfolds, she becomes for the protagonist an object of respect and compassion, a compassion that extends even to her dog, despite the Egyptian's profound fear of dogs and his resentment of the attention lavished on them in the affluent society of his adopted country.

Like this story, many of Taher's writings are about reconciling human differences across boundaries of culture, nationality, and ideology. Taher proposes no facile solutions to the persistent divisiveness of human society. Nevertheless, his stories and novels—peopled as they often are by diverse characters whose improbable alliances are as compelling as they are unusual—bespeak the author's commitment to the idea that differences may be resolved, boundaries transcended.

As to specific themes in Taher's works, these naturally reflect to a considerable degree his own experiences: first of all as an Egyptian in Egypt, during periods of transition and upheaval under both Nasser (1954–70) and Sadat (1970–81); later as an Egyptian living abroad (under virtual exile) in a Western country; and finally as an Egyptian returning—in spirit if not actuality—to the land of his birth.

A striking feature in Taher's writing is the recurrence of ancient Egyptian symbols and themes. Several of his protagonists, in seeking to understand themselves and their experiences, encounter aspects of pharaonic Egypt, whether in dreams, through desert wanderings, or by other means.* The regular repetition of this motif stresses the idea that the identity of the modern Egyptian is inseparably linked to Egypt's ancient culture. A number of Taher's literary works following his move to Switzerland (such as the story described above) deal with the gaps in understanding between Eastern and Western cultures, from the point of view of a displaced Egyptian trying to adjust to life in European society. These pieces express a sense of alienation from both the homeland and the adopted country, and simultaneously a striving toward reconciliation with the homeland and with the adopted country as well.

Aunt Safiyya and the Monastery, which Taher in fact dedicates to his country—as well as to his two daughters—is preceded by

*One of the short stories ("The Trial of the Priest Kai-Nun") is set in the fourteenth century B.C. and concerns a priest accused of heresy for maintaining his adherence to the pacifist ideals and sun-god theology of the Pharaoh Akhenaton, even after the succession of Tutankhamun and the reversion to worship of Amun and the other old gods. The revolutionary monotheistic vision of Akhenaton had not been widely accepted, and its subsequent repudiation under his successor Tutankhamun led to the persecution of Akhenaton's remaining followers.

East of the Palm (first published in its entirety in 1985) and *Duha Said* (also published in 1985). In each of the two earlier novels, the narrator is a young man coming of age in Egypt, trying to establish his identity as an Egyptian and an Arab in an atmosphere of political and societal confusion and angst. Both characters are frustrated with the status quo and disillusioned with a society that offers them little in the way of future prospects or opportunities for self-expression. In some respects, these novels are thematically reminiscent of the stories Taher wrote in the 1960s; but they speak much more directly to such questions as the Palestinian cause and Egypt's ongoing struggle with Israel, as well as to the effect of these issues on Egyptian morale, which is explored in depth through the transformations experienced by the central characters as they grapple with their problems.

The narrator of *Aunt Safiyya and the Monastery* is a man approaching middle age, looking back on a period of his childhood. His story is in part sentimental reminiscence, but it is also much more than that, for the storyteller's narrative depicts a tragedy whose repercussions disrupt the pattern of life in his village, bringing about profound and unexpected changes. All this is set clearly in the broader context of the events surrounding the Arab-Israeli hostilities, and in particular the war of 1967. The novel also implicitly concerns itself with the problem of sectarian relations within Egypt.

It is no coincidence that Bahaa' Taher's *Aunt Safiyya and the Monastery* made its initial appearance at a time of increasingly frequent eruptions of communal strife between Muslims and Copts, when tension was rising throughout Egypt in part because of these incidents. This period—the late 1980s to mid-

1990s—is not the first in which Muslim and Coptic groups have come into conflict; indeed, this is a recurring phenomenon that can be seen as symptomatic of other divisive influences affecting Egyptian society as a whole. Here it is helpful to be at least moderately conversant with the history of the Copts in Egypt and the way in which Muslim-Coptic relations have developed since the Islamicization of that country.

The identification of the Copts as a distinct religious group was an outgrowth of a confusing controversy concerning the nature of Christ that rocked Christianity in the fourth and fifth centuries. The main participants in the dispute were the Orthodox Church itself and two other groups, known as the Nestorians and the Monophysites. The Monophysites lived mainly in Egypt, Syria, and Armenia, and those who dwelled in Egypt were known as Copts. The Monophysites argued that the nature of Christ was wholly divine, whereas the Nestorians maintained that Christ had two entirely discrete natures, one divine and one human. Officials of the Orthodox Church, who held a position midway between the two, persecuted both dissenting groups.

Under Byzantine rule, the Copts continued to suffer persecution from the Orthodox Church. But in the seventh century, the Arab conquest spread from the Arabian peninsula to Egypt: under the leadership of Amr Ibn al-As, the Arabs wrested Egypt from the Byzantine empire. Many Copts at this time saw in the relatively tolerant Muslim government of Amr Ibn al-As an attractive alternative to Byzantine oppression, and thus they readily converted to Islam. Nevertheless, the Coptic community did not disappear but has survived to this day as a distinct religious minority in Egypt, with a strong communal identity. The Copts' sense of identity rests partially in the common belief that they, as distinct from the Arabs whose ancestors invaded Egypt, are the true descendants of the Pharaohs.*

The question of identity—Coptic, Muslim, Egyptian—is a complex one, yet it is arguably *not* primarily the issue of religious identity that has historically given rise to conflict between Muslim and Coptic communities. In fact, the most serious trouble between Coptic and Muslim groups has occurred at times when external or internal political forces have disrupted Egypt's social fabric to such a degree that its citizens have found themselves in a struggle to assert their identity as *Egyptians.* Egypt has many times been challenged in this way, whether as the result of an East-West power struggle, as during the British occupation from 1882 to 1922 and after the 1967 war in which Israel (with the support of Western powers) occupied Sinai, or because the government has failed to serve the needs of the majority of the population—as is currently the case.

It is certainly true that the Copts, owing to their minority status following the establishment of Islam in Egypt, have suffered a certain amount of hardship and persecution—sometimes quite severe—over the course of the centuries leading up to our

*The word "Copt" is itself related to our word "Egypt," which comes from the Greek name for that country. The Greeks called it *Aigyptos,* which is in turn derived from the ancient Egyptian word *Hikuptah.* These are the antecedents of the Arabic word for Copt: *qibt.* (Entirely unrelated to this is the Arabic word for Egypt: *Misr.*) The Coptic language, now restricted to liturgical use, is based on an ancient Egyptian dialect and written in a variant of Greek script.

own.* During the last hundred years, however, recurrent confrontations have reached unprecedented levels of violence. During the British occupation both Copts and Muslims felt disempowered as a result of the British co-optation of government authority. The nationalist movement taken over by Mustafa Kamil in 1906 attempted to unite Egyptians, without reference to religious identity, against the British occupiers. But the Copts, fearing the development of pan-Islamic tendencies in the Muslim-led nationalist movement, had their own agenda. Perceiving themselves now as a minority threatened specifically by the Muslim majority, they sought to advance their own interests under British protection. Consequently, tension between Muslim and Coptic communities rose sharply, as each group strove to assert its place in society and politics. Although a nominal truce was achieved when Copts and Muslims came together in Cairo to try to resolve their differences at the General Egyptian Congress of 1911, the fact remains that what had previously been, for the most part, a cooperative relationship between the two groups had now become a decidedly competitive one, sowing the seeds of a mutual mistrust that has plagued the two communities ever since.

One effect of Egypt's loss in the war of 1967 was an extremist Islamic backlash that, by the time Anwar Sadat came to power in 1970, had reached a degree of intolerance threatening to the Copts. Although in the early years of his presidency Sadat tried

*Between 1012 and 1015 a Muslim leader, the caliph al-Hakim, sometimes described as insane, ruthlessly persecuted the Copts; he was succeeded, however, by al-Zahir, a caliph whose tolerance extended to allowing Copts who had been forced to convert to Islam to resume their Christian faith.

to work with at least some of the Islamic groups, his ultimate response to the conflict between Muslims and Copts was not to mediate disputes but to crack down harshly on both sides, thus further aggravating an already tense situation; violent clashes between the two groups escalated during the years leading up to and following his assassination in 1981.

Conditions in Egypt today are in some respects similar to those of the period just after the 1967 war, although the immediate causes are somewhat different. The country's population has expanded to well beyond what it can comfortably support. Meanwhile, high unemployment increasingly leads those who can to seek work outside Egypt, draining the country of crucial human resources for which the imported income does not adequately compensate. To some extent, the latter problem can be traced to the mid-1970s, when the first major waves of emigration began after Sadat's policies failed to reverse Egypt's economic decline.

The large-scale emigration of highly qualified workers from a country whose population can no longer maintain itself is a vicious circle from which Egypt has so far not managed to escape. As if that were not enough, Egypt—not unlike the other Arab states that were involved—has never fully recovered from the 1967 war (despite the Arabs' relative success in the subsequent confrontation of 1973). Already strained by the series of Arab-Israeli clashes that had come before, Egypt after 1967 was left economically depleted and thoroughly demoralized by the loss of Sinai—as well as the loss of thousands of Egyptian lives. Sinai it has regained, but at a bitter price, for the "separate peace" between Egypt and Israel that was the outcome of the Camp David Accords in 1979 incurred the censure of the Arab states whose lands were not restored by that agreement and the alienation of the Egyptians from many of their fellow Arabs.

The intensity of the conflict between Arabs (both Muslim and Christian) and Israeli Jews that has characterized relations between Israel and its Arab inhabitants and neighbors ever since its founding in 1948 has been a major cause of the rise of violent fringe groups on all sides. Islamic extremists in Egypt have gained a still firmer foothold in a society composed chiefly of Muslims, most of whom are poor and whose basic needs are increasingly desperate and not effectively addressed by the present administration. Like any group seeking political power, these extremist factions promise the populace what the government does not deliver, at the same time profiting from their own identification with the more moderate Islamic groups that are in fact setting up free schools and health-care facilities in some of the regions where such resources are lacking.

Under the circumstances—and I have here touched on only a few of the problems that are straining the social fabric of Egypt—it is easy to understand how certain elements of the society have become polarized. The question of whether such polarization has occurred along religious, ethnic, or political lines, or some combination thereof, is perhaps less significant than the undeniable fact of the resulting social schism. For Egypt has become, in some sense, divided against itself: not only because Muslims and Copts are all Egyptians and some of them are fighting among themselves, but also because on both sides it is, as usual, a volatile minority that is causing most of the disruption, to the grief and consternation of the majority of the populace, regardless of religious affiliation.

This situation is easily enough distorted and misrepresented by the reports that circulate within Egypt itself, as well as in the surrounding Arab countries. Still, it is perhaps most profoundly misunderstood in the West, where the whole Arab-Islamic world is often viewed as a hotbed of religious extremism in which reason and discourse are scarce, while irrational violence, perpetrated mainly on the innocent, is the order of the day. Too little recognition is accorded the voices arguing for peace and for tolerance among different groups—and yet these voices represent the vast majority. And they include Bahaa' Taher. For just as it is no accident that his novel—about a remarkable alliance between a Muslim village in Upper Egypt and the inhabitants of a nearby Coptic monastery—emerges precisely when it does, it is no coincidence that the novel has not just one chief heroic figure, but two: the one a Muslim and the other a Copt.

The novel's protagonist, in the literal sense of "the leading actor," is the father of the narrator. He is a meditative and deeply principled man, a social and religious leader in his community. The mystical hero of the tale is a Coptic monk, who, while often a comic figure who confuses his facts, yet manages to combine humility and authority. He seems to be endowed with extraordinary powers of perception, almost a sixth sense, and in fact as events unfold he emerges as something of a prophet. The Safiyya of the novel's title is also a sympathetic character, but if the narrator's father and the Coptic monk may be said to represent reason and compassion, Safiyya stands for something more primal. For although she is a figure of power and intelligence, what chiefly motivates Safiyya is violent emotion, which takes the form of a savage obsession with the fulfillment of a vengeance to which—according to tradition, not religious principle—she considers herself entitled.

The story takes place in postrevolutionary Egypt, in a small village near Luxor, over a period of years prior to and just after the Arab-Israeli War of 1967. The events are set in motion by an unpremeditated killing within the village's Muslim community, which leads to a blood feud condoned by some members of that community and opposed by others. It is not just the characters themselves that are at variance with one another, but cultural values as well, for those who oppose the blood feud set themselves up in opposition to an ancient and deeply embedded practice. The morality of this custom of exacting blood for blood is not explicitly debated in the novel: both sides of the question are represented by sympathetic characters, whose stories are told. What is particularly interesting, however, is that the opposition to the blood feud brings Muslim and Copt in this novel into a state of true, interdependent symbiosis. Thus on the one hand the feud divides the villagers—all Muslims and all related to one another, whether closely or distantly—while on the other hand the effort to prevent the feud from reaching its bloody conclusion forges a still more powerful bond between two religiously and socially distinct groups already coexisting peacefully in an atmosphere of mutual tolerance and good will.

To suggest that the message here is that all differences can be transcended by opposition to violence would be a vast oversimplification: the dynamics of conflict are more subtle than that. For the response of the Egyptian populace to the Israeli occupation of Palestine, and to Israel's takeover of Sinai in 1967, is quite realistically portrayed in the novel, and this response was by no means one that called for a peaceful solution to the Arab-Israeli conflict. On the contrary, it demanded immediate military mobilization against Israel, and in the strongest possible terms. Moreover, vehement objection to the Israeli seizure of Arab lands is clearly expressed by both Copt and Muslim in this story. Here too is an implicit argument for unification of Egypt's disparate elements through recognition of common interests, but it is an argument of a rather different sort. In this case, Egyptians are called upon to unite against a common enemy, rather than against a violent and divisive tradition.

It is clear then that the enemy of Egypt is not its own peoples, be they Muslim or Christian; rather the enemy is whatever divides Egypt against itself, whether this be an aggressive foreign power that appropriates its land, or, on a more microcosmic level, a destructive practice that sets brother against brother in a tiny Egyptian village. It is this crucial message that I believe the storyteller Bahaa' Taher wishes his novel *Aunt Safiyya and the Monastery* to convey to his readers.

Barbara Romaine
October 1995

Aunt Safiyya and the Monastery

CHAPTER ONE

The Miqaddis Bishai

From the southernmost house in the village, it would take you about half an hour to reach the monastery on foot, and a good deal less than that on the back of a mount. The monastery could not be seen from any part of the village, though—not even from the roof of our house, which was the outermost one. The name by which we knew it was the "Eastern Monastery," for to get there you would head east from the outskirts of the village on a dirt road, and across the desert until you reached the "mountain," as the villagers would refer to those stony brown hills. There you would find, in the lap of the hills, the monastery, with its high walls whose color matched that of the surrounding rocks.

Since ours was the house closest to the monastery, we were in some sense its neighbors. The monks used to give us, in season, sugared dates of a variety known for its small pits, not produced by any of the date palms in our village, but only by those found on the monastery farm. In my boyhood—more than thirty years ago—my father used to take me along with him on Palm Sunday and on the 7th of January—the Coptic Christmas—to offer holiday greetings to the monks. Among the boxes packed with cookies that my mother used to charge me with delivering on the occasion of our Lesser Feast was "the monastery's box." Each time one of us bought new shoes, she used to save carefully those white rectangular shoe-boxes, storing them away during the year. She would get them out at the end of Ramadan and shake the dust off them in preparation for using them. By dawn on the day of the holiday, she would have lined the bottom of each box with cookies sprinkled with sugar, on top of which she placed a thin layer of ghurayyiba, exceptionally light and delicate, with a clove stuck into the middle of each one; she would lay a sheet of thin paper between the layers, place the covers on the cardboard boxes, and begin counting: "A box for your aunt Safiyya, a box for your grandfather Abu Rahab, a box for your uncle Abdel Rahman, a box for . . . and a box for . . . and a box for . . . who have I forgotten?" It didn't much matter to me whom my mother had forgotten, since what it meant was that when she remembered someone she had left out, at that hour of the holiday morning, one of my sisters would take an additional tray of cookies to some of our distant relatives. As for the important gifts, the ones packed in those convenient white boxes, they were a responsibility given only to me, on account of my status as a man in the family. This saved me from the hazards my sisters risked when one of them dropped a tray in the road, so that the cookies were smashed and the expensive ghurayyiba crumbled to pieces in the dust. The girl would return home with all this, in tears, and my mother would receive her with blows and kicks for her unforgivable clumsiness, all the while bewailing the bad luck that had cursed her with the birth of such daughters.

In general, I would finish all my deliveries in the morning after the holiday prayer, saving the monastery's box until early afternoon, so that I could feel free to take my time. For it was my privilege on that day to ride our comfortably saddled white donkey, which, under normal circumstances, was my father's prerogative. When I arrived at the entrance to the monastery, the miqaddis Bishai would open for me the low gate that was barely discernible in the blank wall, beaming and greeting me with the words, "Welcome, distinguished scholar! Welcome, son of our esteemed hagg. Welcome, good neighbor." He was at least as welcoming to the donkey as he was to me, if not more so. He patted the animal's neck, speaking to it gently and indulgently, and all but kissing it. The miqaddis's behavior took me by surprise the first time I went to the monastery on my own, and I asked him why he treated the donkey that way. In a tone of slight reproach, he said, "How can you ask me that, my boy, and you a student at the school? Didn't our Savior enter Jerusalem mounted on a donkey like this one, while the people cheered him?" At that time I understood none of this except for the word "enter," but before I could ask him for any explanation, he surprised me with another riddle. Laughing with some embarrassment, hiding his mouth with one hand and holding the donkey's neck with the other, he said, "My boy, when I made the pilgrimage to Jerusalem, I wished I could ride a donkey like this one, following the way taken by our blessed Savior and the holy family from Egypt to Jerusalem, instead of riding the train to Palestine." Suddenly he remembered something that made him let go of the donkey and begin toying with his beard, frowning. Then he said, as if talking to himself, "Thank God I made the pilgrimage before they took Palestine—may God curse them! If I had waited until now, I wouldn't have been able to get there either on a donkey's back or by train. No, I'd have had to go to east Jordan . . ." Then he raised his face and his hand toward the sky, and said as if he were praying, "May God grant victory to Nasser and drive them from Jerusalem, as he drove the British from Egypt."

After that he turned to me and explained: "This East Jordan, my boy, is a country very far from here. They travel by plane to get there, and your uncle Bishai is afraid . . ." As he said this, his features once again relaxed, and he began to laugh his loud, continuous laughter.

I was about twelve years old then. I had completed elementary school and entered preparatory school, and thought I was supposed to know everything.* So I kept quiet, and didn't ask about things I didn't understand. At that time I remembered what the villagers—and even some of the monks, when they were annoyed with him—used to say about the miqaddis Bishai: that he was "feebleminded." But for all that, the miqaddis Bishai was, of all those who lived in the monastery, the best known in the village, even if we didn't quite know what to make of him. For he wasn't like the other monks, who mostly shut themselves away in the little rooms where they used to worship in private, which were called "qallayaat" or, in the dialect of Upper Egypt, "gallayaat." He used to wear a long, black robe just like the rest of them, but on his head he wore an ordi-

*Preparatory school in Egypt comprises a three-year period between primary and secondary school.

nary skullcap, rather than the cowl turned up at the hem. So was he a monk still in training, or merely a caretaker for the church, or a farmer on the monastery land? No one knew the answer, although his was a well-known face in our little village, and in the neighboring villages as well: he knew everyone and everyone knew him. He was the one who went shopping in Luxor once a week. He would usually go on foot and return in the evening, carrying on his back and in his hands sacks of sugar, rice, tea, kerosene tanks and reflectors for the lanterns, and all the other things that the monastery needed. Very often, as he made his way, the farmworkers would stop him, and, there in the middle of their fields, ask him questions about farming; or he might stop of his own accord to give his opinion and advice. If he passed through the irrigated lands and found that a farmer had planted his lentils, and the earth was too soggy, he would scold him, saying, "You there, why have you planted these lentils before the right time? Be careful how you water them. Don't drown them, or they won't grow well. Don't you know that lentils don't like water?"

It was well known that his advice on planting was never wrong, whatever might be said about the feebleness of his mind. There were those who believed that it was his communication with the spirits that gave him this special skill—but that's what they always say about anyone who doesn't talk like the rest of us, or whose behavior seems eccentric. And so they would mutter fearfully, "God protect us from evil." Not only that, but a few of these mutterers were afraid he could cast the evil eye on their crops, because all of his predictions came true.

My father, on the other hand, laughed at such muttering, and said that those people were more feebleminded than the miqaddis Bishai. He also said that Bishai knew a great many secrets from farming the sandy and ungiving monastery ground, and for this reason, my father was always eager to consult him before planting.

The year of the cotton craze in our village, when all the farmers took to comparing the yields from cotton with the sparse yields from the lentils, the miqaddis Bishai said to my father with a laugh, "Cotton, ya hagg? What cotton, in this land of ours, where you could work yourself to death just trying to grow a patch of weeds? Better to grow corn." My father did not take this as a joke. He consulted Harbi as well, who was the closest of our relatives and the most skillful farmer in the village. Harbi told him, "Don't listen to what people say, son of my father. Plant cotton in this ground? Those people—'their papers have gone north.'"

He meant by this that these people were hopeless cases, or had gone wrong in the head, and were in for serious trouble. For someone whose official papers had been sent north to Cairo could only expect to end up in jail or an insane asylum. So when the cotton crop failed—the short stems withering and the bolls turning out smaller than chickpeas—everyone who had been taken in by the idea of planting cotton and the stories of its advantages was kicking himself for doing so. My father, though, praised God that he had been satisfied with what little he had, and that he had taken the advice that came his way.

But I haven't explained why it was that I enjoyed going to the monastery by myself at ʿEid, even after I had started preparatory school and become a person who could be taken seriously. The truth is that first of all I was happy to be by myself. For when I went with my father, I had to sit quietly while he talked to the monks, and all the time he would watch my movements from the corner of his eye. For instance, I had to finish every drop of the honeyed drink they offered us at the monastery, although I did not like it, and I was not allowed to make any noise while I drank it. (Naturally, I could not point out to my father that he himself, as well as the monks, made great loud slurping sounds with every sip.) When I had finished my drink, I had to get up and put the cup on the tray myself, saying clearly, "Thank you very much," after which I was still not allowed to take part in the adults' conversation, or to move from my place until we left together, with him holding my hand.

But at ʿEid, I could do as I liked, once I had delivered the box of cookies to the monastery and received the monks' holiday greetings, to be conveyed to my father along with their thanks for his endless efforts, and their wishes that the Lord make him always prosperous . . . and so on, and so on. On that day I was free to explore the monastery. It somewhat resembled our village, with its winding passageways and its houses—or cells—built of mud-brick that differed from ours only in their domed roofs. I could go with the miqaddis Bishai to the monastery farm. This reached from the cells all the way to the mountain. There was a high wall separating the farm from the monastery buildings. It was an extension of the great wall that enclosed all the buildings, and had a small gate leading into the monastery and the farm. The wall that enclosed the farm itself was not as high or as thick as the main wall. In the middle of the farm wall, on the side facing the village, was a large double-leafed gate of thick wood. This opened to admit the donkeys, so that the harvest could be brought in. In the middle of the farm was a little reed hut, surrounded by small date palms that always shaded it.

It was there that the miqaddis Bishai lived most of the time. I used to enjoy the rounds of strong tea that he would offer me, one cup after another, while he told his endless stories of the things he had seen in the village since he came to the monastery as a very young man, forty years earlier.

He could never sit still when he was talking, but was always doing something: he would go and give orders to the monks who were helping him with the planting, or he would pull weeds from among the crops, or trim one of the trees, or level the ground with his hoe, and all the while he would never stop his talking and laughing. He wouldn't get angry when I laughed at his bizarre stories, but would put his hand on his chest and say with a smile, "Tomorrow you'll see that your uncle Bishai was right!"

The miqaddis Bishai was as proud of the story of our village as if he had been one of its founders. To be sure, he had not witnessed the events from the beginning, but he had been told things by the late Bakhoum. This Bakhoum had lived past the age of a hundred. Bishai used to follow him around here and there, when he first came to the monastery as a novice, in his youth. So he knew that our village had originally been uncultivated land that lay between the crown estates to the north and Luxor to the south; and that our ancestors who built the village were farmworkers who had fled the persecution and oppression of life on the estates. Then they had prepared for cultivation the land that lay near the monastery, each man owning just as much land as he could farm himself. For this reason, no one in the village was wealthy, in the usual sense of the word. The only one of our ancestors who amassed a fortune was Asran-bey, who had been able to buy land next to the field he tilled. Asran's family remained for a time the richest in the village, and was the family to whose oldest members the rank of mayor passed, even though after two or three generations they had become like the majority of the villagers: in other words, they had joined the ranks of the poor and those who were just getting by, like us. We too were from a branch of Asran's family; in fact we were tied to all the other families of the village, all of whom were related to one another by marriage. This didn't prevent blood feuds between some of the families. It's true that such feuds were less common among our people than in the neighboring villages, but they were no less violent.

Sometimes I used to try to correct the miqaddis Bishai when he recounted to me the history of the village, but I never got anywhere with that, and neither did anyone else. He clung stubbornly to the ideas he had formed when he heard the tales from the late Bakhoum. A tear would fall from his eye any time he mentioned the name of his mentor. Usually the miqaddis Bishai would end his stories by saying, "The people of this village are free, my boy, and they don't put up with abuse, not even if . . ." Then he would become too self-conscious to reveal to me what should have followed that "not even if."

In this way, I used to spend an hour or more with him in his compound on the monastery farm. Then we would go back the way we had come, through the little gate and into the monastery proper. Before I left, we would go up to the rectangular hall that differed from all the other monastery buildings in its raised ceiling and its high, round windows placed directly below the ceiling and resembling the openings of pigeon houses. This room was always cool, even in the heat of the day. The hall also housed the monastery's collection of antiquities: painted portraits and plants sketched on the old timbers, on pieces of cloth, and on the fragments of broken stone affixed to the wall beside the small statues that were scattered about. At that age I was drawn only to the perpetually sad, bearded faces, with the gilded haloes that encircled their heads, and to the pictures of the white-winged angels whose bright haloes, looking like hoops, appeared a bit above their heads.

I had heard the story of this hall from the monks. The miqaddis Bishai had told it to me a number of times with much enthusiasm . . . Long ago, a European had visited the monastery. When he came across the paintings and statues piled up in one of the underground storage areas, he donated money for the construction of this hall and sent an architect from Cairo to build it. This was unheard of, since the village houses and the monastic cells, too, were always erected by the locals themselves, with the help of skilled farmworkers' building expertise. As for architects, we had never heard of them until after the airport was built. But Bishai used to say that the man who had built this hall was an architect, and that he had designed the building in such a way that it would stay cool all year round, so that the paintings would not dissolve in the heat. Bishai would add, stressing his words, "Believe me, my boy . . . he was a genuine architect from Cairo—that's what Bakhoum told me, God rest his soul." This generous European, who had made a donation for the construction of the hall, was always referred to by the miqaddis Bishai as "Kabb el-Noor Abu-shaʿr Sayeh."* The monks had become fed up with him in their attempts to teach

*Literally, "flowing-haired spiller-of-light"—*kabb* is a verb that may be construed as meaning "to spill."

him the correct version of the name, and I had likewise given up trying to find out what it was really supposed to be. One time, one of the monks corrected him when I was there. The monk was rather irritated, and said with a mocking laugh, "Who is this 'Kabb el-Noor'? And just what did he 'kabb,' ya Bishai, you ignoramus? I've told you a hundred times, his name was Kabalour Abu-shaʿr Sayeh!" Another monk said—almost in a whisper, but with conviction—"No, it was Columbar Abu-shaʿr Sayeh."

I asked Brother Girgis, who was well educated: he had spent time at the American school in Asyut at the time my father was studying at the religious academy there, and they had become friends. He told me with a smile, "Son, I don't know any 'Spiller-of-light' or 'Spiller-of-waters,' or Kabalour, or Columbar. All I know is an old newspaper photograph of him with Bakhoum—God rest his soul. His hair was parted in the middle and hung down on both sides of his face." I asked him, "Where is that picture now?" He pointed his finger toward the sky and said, "God only knows."

Some time later, after I started attending high school, I thought I had solved this mystery, and I asked my father if he had heard about a certain Lord Cromer, who had visited our village and the monastery. My father replied irritably, "Clomer who, boy? Has somebody told you I'm head watchman at the village gate, and I count every khawaaga who comes and goes? Now get out of here—go study something useful, and quit gossiping about people!"

So I never did find out. No one ever explained to me who it was that had built this strange hall that was always cool, in the heart of the desert. It too was made of mud-brick—like the rest of the cells and all the other buildings in the monastery except for the church and the wall—but its outer wall was daubed with white lime, most of which had gradually fallen away. What remained clung in patches to the mud-brick, like painted figures.

I remember the first time I entered that hall with the miqaddis Bishai. He stopped in front of a picture of the Virgin, who held the Christ child on her lap and gazed down at him. Bishai began suddenly to sing in a hoarse voice: "Oh, Mother of the Light, oh . . ." His song echoed in the shadowy hall. Then his voice began to tremble and he nearly wept as he sang,

Oh, teach us to be thankful,
The Almighty glorify,
With humble hearts to worship
Our all-seeing Lord on high . . .

I found myself staring in surprise at his downcast face, and his eyes, wide and glistening with tears. Before my eyes he began to resemble those sad faces drawn on the stones and cracked timbers that surrounded us. I decided to leave him there and go outside, but the miqaddis Bishai stopped singing as suddenly as he had started. The smile returned to his face, while the tears still stood in his eyes. He said to me, squinting and cocking his head as was his way, "But suppose his name really was 'Spiller-of-light'? . . . Bakhoum—may he rest in peace—told me: this world is dark, and the light is there above. But he who does something here on earth . . . can't he spill a bit of the light from heaven onto the earth?"

Then he hesitated for a moment, having lost his train of thought. He stood scratching his forehead, and he laughed his loud laugh. "Excuse me a moment," he said. Then he went to a corner of the hall, picked up a small broom, and began sweeping the floor, raising clouds of dust. I stood waiting by the door. He spoke up clearly then, his voice once again tinged with sorrow. "Look," he said, "even you, a young pupil, of a different religion from ours—even you are drawn to these pictures and you like to gaze at them. Meanwhile, these foreign tourists who come from the ends of the earth to mill around, pushing and shoving and practically killing themselves in the heat and the sun just to get a look at statues of heathen gods in the temples of Luxor . . . not one of them has the decency to come here and look at the pictures of the immaculate Virgin. And they call themselves Christians!"

He had stopped sweeping. He stood up straight, placing a hand on his back. He sighed, and said, in strong Saʿiidi, *"Gabr yakhudhum kulluhum!"**

In our village, this expression was not so harsh as it sounds, for it was used in expressions of anger and pleasure alike, or simply as a joke, or possibly for no particular reason at all, like "Good morning" and "Good evening."

In any case, the miqaddis Bishai was the last person who would wish harm on anyone. I saw him with my own eyes one day, weeping as he bandaged the leg of an injured rabbit on the monastery farm, dressing it with cotton and muslin. In those days, we only saw things like that in hospitals. For us, the most extreme treatment for a wound was to dab it with ground coffee beans; most of the time, we would simply leave wounds to be healed by exposure to the sun.

* *Qabr yakhudhum kulluhum!* "May the grave take them all!"

CHAPTER TWO

Aunt Safiyya

Delivery of the monastery's box of cookies was the last of my errands on the morning of ʿEid. After I got back, the real holiday would begin, when I would get together with my relatives and friends and we would start our games. We might decide to go to Luxor, to ride bicycles whose frames were decorated with colored paper. And we would go to the movies.

As for the first box, this one I carried happily, in a hurry to arrive, for this was of course the box for my aunt Safiyya. I used to look forward to a generous holiday present and a firm invitation to stay with her awhile. Aunt Safiyya wasn't more than seven or eight years older than I, as she wasn't actually my aunt. I thought she was the most beautiful human being in the world, excepting only Faten Hamama,* whom I had fallen in

*Popular Egyptian actress, whose career began in the 1940s, when she was still a young girl.

love with the very first time I saw one of her films at the Luxor cinema. The happiest moments of my childhood were when Aunt Safiyya would hug me, and I would smell the scent of the jasmine perfume with which she doused herself. That was in the old days, when she still used perfume. Later, though, in the days when I used to bring her a box of cookies at ʿEid, I was pursued by my mother's words of warning, which she would keep repeating over and over at the same time she encouraged me: "I know you're a clever boy, I know you won't disgrace me. Now, what are you going to say? You're going to say, 'This box is for Hassaan.' Don't you dare say, 'My mother sends you this box.' And how are you going to enter the house?" "Without any fuss," I would answer my mother. "Exactly," she would say, "exactly. Smart boy. And mind you don't look too cheerful or say, 'Happy holidays,' or any such thing. Just go in, greet your aunt, and if Hassaan is awake, give him the box without saying anything, or put it to one side without a word." Then my mother would bite her lip, perhaps brushing away a tear, and say, "Poor Safiyya. Her day of celebration is still a long way off."

Aunt Safiyya and I were brought up together in the same house. I thought of her as I thought of my four sisters. We were all younger than she, except for the firstborn, Ward es-Sham (whom my father had named after his grandmother, as a sign of respect). But my mother had taught me from an early age to call Safiyya "Aunt." She was actually my mother's cousin on her mother's side. Safiyya's parents had died together in one of the village's recurrent outbreaks of malaria. Since my mother was Safiyya's closest living relative, and my father was paternal first cousin to my mother,* it was only natural that she should come and live with us. Of course, Safiyya was also related to everyone else in the village—like me, like all of us. The fact is that everyone was a close or distant relative of everyone else, on either the paternal or the maternal side, from our first citizen, the mayor Hamid Asran, to the humblest tenant farmer. But we were, as I said before, her closest relatives. Moreover, my father had spent two years at the religious institute in Asyut; he sometimes delivered the Friday sermon in the mosque and he led the people in prayer when our imam was away.† Thus he was a well-respected man among the villagers, and the court judge in Luxor, who was also from our village, had entrusted him with the upbringing of this orphan as well as the disposition of her inheritance.

From the time she was small, Safiyya used to turn heads with her beauty. She was fine featured, with a small mouth and nose. Whenever she cut her hair, it grew right back again and fell down her back, soft and thick, and so long it hung below the black headcloth she wore, which covered her shoulders and back. Her eyes were singularly beautiful: they were not black or brown, but I can't say exactly what color they were. The closest I could come would be to say that, in the shade, they were the color of pale honey; in the sun, or in bright light, those bewitching eyes turned the color of gold, approaching green, but with

*Literally, "the son of my mother's father's brother": Arab familial relationships are much more closely defined than in Western societies; and in traditional Arab cultures, marriages between first cousins are not uncommon.

†In Islam, Friday is the day of public worship.

a mixture of many other colors as well. Very often, as a child, I saw people—men and women—fall silent in midsentence when Aunt Safiyya looked up through her thick lashes at the person with whom she was speaking. After a pause in which no one said anything, they would murmur—so as to ward off the evil eye—*bismillaahi maa shaa' allah.* My mother, likewise fearing the evil eye, after guests had gone home would frequently recite incantations over Safiyya and perfume her with incense, to protect her. This roused the jealousy of my sisters, even though they loved Safiyya as much as I did: they were always putting their arms about her neck and kissing her. I was not allowed to do this, since my parents considered me from the age of six almost a man, who must avoid playing with girls, and with my aunt Safiyya in particular.

Just as Aunt Safiyya was the loveliest of girls, my paternal uncle Harbi was the most handsome of men. He was a distant cousin of my father on his father's side. He too was an orphan. His land was next to ours, and he and my father often joined efforts in cultivating both plots. Harbi was constantly at our house, and my father—who was his mother's only son—thought of him as a younger brother. So did my mother, who also used to call him by the name that siblings often used with each other: "son of my father."

Although Safiyya's suitors began flocking to my father from the time she was about ten years old, he stated firmly that he would not think of marrying her off before she had come of legal age, which at that time was fourteen. My father also wanted Aunt Safiyya to be educated, like my sisters, who at his insistence were required to finish at least primary school. My mother, however, who had grudgingly accepted my father's wishes in the matter of my sisters' attending school, could not wait for Safiyya to complete even one year before she put her foot down: she insisted that Safiyya stay at home. She said that she was barely able to protect Safiyya from the evil eye when the girl was confined to the house, so what was she to do if Safiyya was going out every day where any good-for-nothing who wanted to could look at her? "The child has an unlucky star," said my mother. "She's an easy target for the evil eye. Since she started school, she's come down with all kinds of aches and pains." Because my mother considered Safiyya her personal responsibility, my father let her have her way, and so Safiyya stayed at home. But my sisters Ward es-Sham, Sikeena, and Ruqayya got no such privileges, for all their tears and their begging: they didn't have an unlucky star, and my father was stubborn.

All the same, Safiyya's age and the matter of her education were not the only reasons my father turned away her suitors. Above all else was the belief, both in our household and in the rest of the village, that Safiyya was for Harbi, though he had never asked my father for her hand. In fact, he treated her just the way he treated my sisters: as a child.

Harbi was tall, with golden-brown skin. In his cheeks were two ruddy circles; these were set off by his black moustache, its ends always carefully twisted to a point, which made him all the more handsome. His Adam's apple was prominent in his long neck, and it moved visibly up and down any time he talked or sang. In fact, his strong voice was his best feature. We all knew that, and we were always after him to sing at weddings and parties; or he might spontaneously volunteer, as a favor to the host of the occasion. He sang local folk songs such as "*ʿabbadi ya wad,*

ʿabbadi," * or *"rann ilkhilkhaal ʿa-ssillim sahhani."* † Or he might improvise, adding to the common collection of songs one that praised the host of the party or event.

Harbi's relationship with the gypsy girl, the golden-haired Amuna el-Baida el-Halabiyya—who danced at weddings—was well known. And everyone knew that she loved him to the exclusion of all those many men who would have liked to get close to her. Once, at a wedding, she made up a song, which quickly became known in the village. When Harbi appeared in their midst, the men would sing it, smiling and winking and raising their voices, "My heart was confounded, my heart was confused, but on the day I met him, it was troubled no more . . ."‡ Harbi would smile back at the men and joke along with them without embarrassment. For at that time, in our village, such relationships were permitted to men who were still unmarried, and even to some unfaithful married men who simply had no self-control. In any case, there was no reason why this relationship should have prevented Harbi from asking for Safiyya's hand, if he had wanted to.

But did Safiyya love Harbi?

I can't say for certain, but I remember from my earliest childhood that she and all my sisters were in the habit of spying

*"Oh handsome boy, handsome boy!" (folk song sung to the groom at weddings in Upper Egypt).

† Literally, "[her] anklet jingled on the stairs and woke me up."

‡ In the Arabic, the first line of this song is a play on words that makes it quite clear Amuna is singing about Harbi. She sings, *"Haar bi qalbi,"* meaning roughly, "My heart was confounded"; but the combination of the first two words is deliberately meant to resemble Harbi's name, so that this line could be taken as having a second meaning, "Harbi is my sweetheart."

on him through half-closed doors when he would sit with my father on the bench in the courtyard, discussing the crops or drinking tea and chatting. I don't remember whether it was Safiyya or one of my sisters whom I overheard—when I surprised them once, sneaking glances at Harbi—saying of him, "Dear God! He's like the rising moon!" I threatened to expose them all before our parents for their brashness, but Aunt Safiyya kissed me on the forehead, asking reproachfully, "Would it make you happy to disgrace me, son of my sister?"

All the resolve in my heart melted on the spot.

I remember another time, when I saw Aunt Safiyya sitting by herself in the courtyard—she and I were the only ones at home—singing softly to herself, "My heart was confounded . . ." Amuna el-Baida's song was actually a lively one, with a dance melody, but there was Aunt Safiyya—crouched on the ground, holding her head in her hands and singing the words slowly, to a sad tune, like a dirge, her body rocking back and forth, back and forth, now to the right, now to the left. When she realized that I was there behind her, she turned around all at once with a strange gleam in her eye and spoke to me in a harsh tone I had never heard her use before: "What are you doing here, boy? Get out of here!" I froze in my place.

At that time, I had not yet started school; but the years passed, I entered primary school, Safiyya came of age, and Harbi still had not asked for her hand. Months went by, then a year, more . . . and my parents had no idea what to do about that silence. It became more and more awkward for my father to answer Safiyya's suitors, but he continued to make excuses to them.

After Safiyya turned sixteen, Harbi came to the house, and with him was the consul-bey.

The consul was the grandson of the great Asran, and like Asran had achieved the rank of a bey in the days when Egypt was still ruled by a king. Although he was the biggest landowner in the village and had the largest house there, he lived in Luxor in a separate house known in our village as "the palace." This house really was as beautiful as a palace. It was built in the oriental style, its front facade and entryway being composed of a series of arches, like an arcade. The furniture inside consisted of wooden chairs, tables, and couches inlaid with shell. There were expensive Persian carpets on the floor, in addition to those hanging on the walls. There was a chandelier hung from the ceiling whose parts were of wrought silver, encasing lamps that were like candles. But the most beautiful section of this house, which I can picture at any time as if it were before my eyes, was the path in the garden. It was lined on both sides by European palm trees with white trunks, like short pillars set at regular intervals. These were connected by a curb covered in blue mosaic tiles, among which were engraved white flowers. This pathway was broad enough so that in its exact middle, it became a circle, in the center of which was a little fountain, whose rim was of the same blue and engraved mosaic. The water came out and fell in little arcs like palm leaves.

The consul-bey was the pride of our village and one of my favorite people in the province when I was a child. He used to wear always, summer and winter, a dark suit and a white shirt and tie, even in the worst heat, and even when he went about the dusty alleyways of our village. Then there was the red tarbush, which no one except him ever wore anymore, after the revolution: it made him even more dignified, in our eyes. He would always fill his pockets with candy and with small change in new silver coins, which he would hand out to the children. He used to present to me at holidays a new pound note with no creases in it—the only pound note that ever came my way. My mother, however, would always confiscate it and give it to me in installments over time, lest I be corrupted by my wealth.

Although the bey had never in his life worked in the diplomatic corps and had never done anything except farming and commerce, he was nevertheless a real consul. I don't know the reason, but somehow, while still a young man, he had managed to claim the status of honorary consul from the kingdom of Greece. The same king who had awarded him this status had also honored him with a medal, which was still there in his house in the village, in its red velvet box. There was also a picture of the consul-bey in his youth, the tarbush on his head and this medal on the breast pocket of his jacket. The photographer had taken pains to use the light in such a way as to make the bey's dark-brown skin appear lighter, his broad mouth less wide—as if the photographer were making the picture into art. For the lower half of the picture was incomplete, while an uneven white halo caused the bey's black jacket to fade out in different places, making the photograph look like a statue bust, cropped so as to show off the medal in all its splendor.

The bey did not change much after the revolution. It's true that he was the only one in the village who was subject to the land reform law, but he had accepted that with equanimity. It was said that some of the farmworkers to whom his lands were distributed went to the bey and told him that the land was his, even if the government had deeded it to them. But the consul refused to hear this kind of talk. He said to them, "This is a blessing bestowed upon you by God, so take advantage of it. What do I need the land for? Who but you will inherit it from me? We're all one family, all related. If you ever need anything, come to me; and if I ever need anything, I'll come to you."

Nevertheless, the bey gave up farming after his holdings were reduced to two hundred feddans. He left it to his sister's son Harbi to oversee the cultivation of the remaining land and to keep accounts for it. Meanwhile, the bey settled in Luxor, where he owned some large wholesale shops. He would send boats to transport goods to and from the Sudan, and he spent the rest of his time putting up buildings in Luxor and Qena—and indeed in Cairo, no less, so it was said. The bey was even able to establish good relations with the officers of the revolution. My father continued to boast for a long time about the day one of the leaders of the revolution, Colonel Salah Saalem—may he rest in peace—had visited the palace with a delegation of leaders from the Sudan. On that day, my father told us, there was an honor guard of soldiers in red berets surrounding the consul's palace.

But the point is that Harbi came to our house, and the consul-bey came with him, so that the bey could ask for Safiyya's hand in marriage for himself.

My father was stunned. He sat staring in silence at the bey, who was past the age of sixty at that time, though he had been twice married and widowed without producing any children. But he said—coming to the rescue of my father, who could not find words to speak—that at his age he must have someone to look after him, and so he had thought of the orphaned girl.

When my father still said nothing, Harbi eagerly pointed out that marriage to the bey would be an honor to any girl and would raise her status. At this point, my father managed to stammer that the consul had honored his house with this visit, and that for such an honor he would be ready to offer up his own neck for the consul, if he asked him to. But as to the girl's marriage, he must consult her. It was no simple matter for my father to refuse the bey directly, as he had refused all her other suitors, and he was trying, with these words, to find a way out. When he had finished speaking, however, Harbi clapped his hands and said, "Then it's settled—thanks be to God! All we have to do is to let the one concerned decide."

My father stood up heavily. At that moment, my mother appeared from inside the house, by herself, carrying a tea tray, on which were a china teapot and some small gold-rimmed cups. These things were never brought out except on very important occasions, such as this visit by the consul. Since her hands were occupied, the veil that—in accordance with tradition—covered my mother's face was held between her teeth, and she was pressing it between her lips. She came slowly forward until she could put down the tea tray on the little table in front of the large armchair on which the bey was seated, and which my father and I had brought from the diwan into the courtyard for this occasion. When my mother had placed the tea before the consul—who, by various ties of either blood or marriage, was her uncle on both sides and her grandfather as well—she approached him, greeted him, and kissed his hand. He let her do this, all the while chuckling quietly. "Greetings," he said, "to my mother-in-law—may the wedding cup be filled to the brim!" My mother looked at Harbi with a radiant smile. "So?" she asked.

"Is this true, Harbi?" My father was afraid she might say something compromising at that moment, and all would be lost. So he took her by the hand, feigning a laugh, and said, *"in shaaʾ allah, in shaaʾ allah."* And with that, he practically dragged her into the house.

Ward es-Sham said later that the color rose in Safiyya's face when my father brought her the news, and she asked him in a soft voice, "Harbi said that?" "Yes," my father replied with a sigh of resignation, "Yes, child, Harbi did say that." My sister said that Safiyya, on hearing this, raised her head: her eyes half-filled her face, and in them was that strange gleam. She said calmly to my father, "Then I agree, Father . . . I will marry the consul, and I'll bear him a son."

Startled, my father replied, "But, daughter . . ."

Aunt Safiyya covered her face with her veil, saying, "As you wish, Father . . . the decision is yours . . . but I am willing to marry the consul-bey."

My father said nothing for a few moments. Then he sighed, and said, "No, the decision is God's." And he went out to tell the bey that Safiyya had accepted his proposal. And so Aunt Safiyya got married, and left our house to live in the palace.

Rumors circulated in the village that Abd el-Wahhab and Umm Kulthoum were to perform at the wedding,* as they had at the bey's two previous weddings, but the consul, maintaining his dignity, laughed and said, "At my age? It's enough that we offer sharbat, and slaughter a lamb to feed the poor."

So I lost all hope of a great wedding for my aunt Safiyya, just as I had lost hope for the marriage itself. For there was no

*Well-known and highly popular Egyptian singers.

drumming or singing, nothing but a dinner at the palace. My mother and sisters and a few female relatives gave out ululations of joy. Harbi danced the "fencing dance" in the palace garden, to melodies performed on a single mizmar. To the consul-bey he sang a well-known song, the lyrics to which he changed so that the last line went, "And our consul is the finest of men."

After the ma'dhoun had left, Aunt Safiyya appeared before us, her closest relatives. She had made up her face with lipstick, rouge, and powder, and she wore a shining white dress that fell to just above her heels. When I saw her, so shy, not knowing what to do with her hands—lacing her fingers together at one moment, then placing one hand over her heart at another—as she wandered among us, her beautiful eyes full of confusion . . . when I saw her so, I hid my face in my hands and cried silently. Then I left the party, and sat by the fountain to be alone with my tears.

But a few days after the wedding, Safiyya began to seem like herself again. How proud my mother was of her! She would say, "I brought her up, and she has done us proud!" She said that the consul-bey had never in his long life known happiness such as Safiyya had given him. She said that Safiyya was at the bey's beck and call. Then she turned to my sisters and said, sounding pained, "Not like these impossible creatures, who sleep until the call for noon prayer!" In this my mother was being unfair to my sisters, who, in spite of their youth and the fact that they went to school five days a week, did all the chores in the house, from making bread and cooking meals to sweeping. But this kind of talk was my mother's way of keeping them in line.

Aunt Safiyya really did do my mother proud, though. For in

the consul's palace, which was filled with servants, Safiyya rose at dawn and did as my mother had always done: she prepared her husband's breakfast with her own hands. Then she would remain standing at his shoulder, ready to fulfill his every request, making sure that he had eaten his fill and that there was nothing missing or out of its proper place. After breakfast, she would have his suit all laid out for him, clean and ironed, with a spotlessly clean white shirt. She herself would help him dress. Then she would see him to the door, brushing any lint or dust from his jacket, or straightening his collar. She would warn the driver to be careful driving the car and to remind the bey when lunch was, in case he got caught up in his work at the office and forgot.

I remain puzzled, even to this day—though I am much older now—by the question: how could Safiyya, after that first beautiful love of hers, so love that man who was more than three times her age? But will I ever happen upon the real answer to this question? Will I find out whether she had a particular reason for loving the bey, or whether she loved him out of a kind of weakness, or whether she simply loved him the way any woman might love any man?

This is what I ask myself now, at this distance in time and place. At the time, though, when I was a child beginning primary school, there was nothing in the world that could inflame my heart with jealousy so much as that strange love, the total devotion with which Safiyya treated the consul-bey. She would weep and turn pale if he was late coming home, and she would send out the house servants, each in a different direction, to look for him. She would not eat a bite if he suffered from so much as a slight cold or a headache, but would sit pale faced beside his bed all day, for as long as he was ill. My mother and the consul-bey would both beg her to eat and sleep a little, but all in vain. Her devotion was unaffected by the passage of time: it stayed firm until the end.

Then came the bey's greatest happiness. One day my mother returned from Luxor, and began—this woman who was always so dignified—to give out ululations of gladness in our house, and she told her daughters to do the same: "My girls," she said to them, "this is the joy of a lifetime . . . a joy I never looked for or expected . . . your aunt Safiyya is pregnant!"

The whole village gathered at our house, and my mother began handing out sharbat and karkadeh. When Harbi heard the news, he came running, seized my father's rifle from where it hung on the wall, and began firing shots in the air and dancing. "Wallahi," he declared, "God has decreed happiness for you, Uncle . . . wallahi, God has rewarded your patience and given back to you full measure for the goodness of your heart!" Then Harbi himself began passing out the sharbat to the men sitting in the diwan. My mother said she had never seen Harbi so happy as he was on that day.

So she said, but it seems the good guys never win in the end, and the devil always gets his due. My mother's eyes fill with tears as she says, "Wallahi, no one on earth has ever been wronged the way Harbi was—served like el-Hasan and el-Hussein, he was!"

So how did it happen that the bey's overpowering joy at the birth of his son Hassaan was surpassed only by his terrible anger at Harbi, who before that had been so dear to him, had been his closest confidant? How did our kindhearted consul, who we had thought could do no wrong, come to drive Harbi from the palace garden and order him never to set foot or show his face there again?

That day, Harbi came to my father in a state of alarm. He begged my father to explain to him what had happened. He swore that even if he himself had married and had a child, he would not have rejoiced as he had for the birth of Hassaan. He said to my father, "If you only knew how much I love the bey, not just as my uncle, but as if he were my father, who died so young, and whom I no longer remember . . . no, I love my uncle more than myself! For who is there that can compare with him, the head of the family . . . the pride of the family?" He declared that he was ready to die to ransom the dust off the bey's shoe. What had happened, he wanted to know? He struck his face with his hands, asking my father again, what had happened to make the bey so angry with him. He took a pistol from his breast pocket and held it out to my father. "Give this to the bey," he said, "so he can shoot me with it if he recalls a single unkind word to him that ever passed my lips. Or shoot me yourself right now if you've ever heard that I wronged the bey in any way."

My father pushed away Harbi's hand that held the pistol. He spoke sadly, saying, "There is no strength or power, except in God . . . no strength or power . . ." Then he turned to me and ordered me to harness the horse to the carriage. This meant he was going to Luxor immediately. But when Harbi tried to go with him, my father told him to stay behind and wait for him.

My father left before noon. Harbi and I sat waiting for him in the diwan outside the house. My father was gone a long time in

Luxor. The whole time, Harbi would not taste even a bite of food. Twice he sent back the tray that my mother had me bring out, without touching the food. He would accept nothing except some tea. He sat cross-legged on the couch, his upper body rocking monotonously back and forth, muttering things too indistinct to be heard or understood. From time to time he turned to me, dazedly repeating the words my father had spoken, "There is no strength or power except in God." He beat his palms one against the other, and his ruddy cheeks grew still more flushed. Every time he heard a sound, or thought he heard a sound, he would leap up and run out toward the street.

But my father stayed away a long time and did not come back until just before sunset. His face was clouded, and he spoke with finality as he jumped down from the carriage. He said to Harbi, who stood there swaying as if he might fall, "Son of my father, leave this matter in God's hands. Forget about the bey for the time being. Perhaps God will set things to rights . . ."

This did not satisfy Harbi. He took hold of my father's arm and begged him to reveal to him the secret of the bey's anger. My father tried in vain to evade Harbi's urgent questions, saying only that some people had come between Harbi and the consul. "Who are these people?" Harbi demanded. "What have they said? Why didn't the bey confront me directly with these accusations? How could the bey believe such slander against me, when I'm the one who has lived his whole life to serve him, without ever demanding anything in return?"

My father was unable to answer all these questions: he didn't know who those people were. The bey had refused every one of my father's requests that he disclose their names. And he didn't know how the consul could believe this slander. He had tried his best to convince the bey that Harbi was innocent, but it was no use.

In the end, in the face of Harbi's insistence—for Harbi had not let go of my father's arm or let up in his questioning—my father came close to losing his patience and getting angry. "Son of my father," he said, "they say that you swore to kill Hassaan in order to claim your inheritance from the bey uncontested. And the consul believes what those damned troublemakers have said, may God have mercy on us all."

Harbi let go of my father's arm and stood staring in horror. Then he turned and walked away without a word. When he had gone quite some way, he turned and came back. My father and I were unharnessing the horse from the carriage. Harbi said in a voice of absolute calm, "And you, son of my father? Do you believe that I said that, or that I would even think of such a thing?"

My father replied wearily, his throat constricted with exhaustion and grief, "No, Harbi. I swore to the consul, on the life of my son here, that you never said any such thing, nor ever thought any such thing. But it was no use."

Harbi said softly, "Thank God."

And he walked away slowly, in silence.

That night, while my parents were having dinner, I heard my father say sadly to my mother, "Even Safiyya believes that Harbi said those things."

My mother replied angrily, "But who spread these lies? God's curse upon him!" My father was quiet for a long time, as if he wanted to think carefully before he spoke. In the same tone as before, he said, "Yes, God's curse upon whoever started this slander." Then he sighed, adding, "An evil thing has begun. If only it would go no further than this."

My father warned me against repeating to anyone a word of what I had heard. But there was no need for me to say anything: after a few days, the whole village was talking about what had happened. A number of people took to defending Harbi, but there were others who poured fuel on the fire. Messages flew back and forth between Luxor and the village. It was said that there were men who had volunteered to stand armed guard over the palace. Such people were among those who were jealous of Harbi because of his long-standing relationship with the bey . . . or were jealous of Harbi simply because he was Harbi. But when the bey saw them standing about the palace like bad news on the doorstep, he drove them off with curses, declaring that he was capable of protecting his own house. All this further inflamed the bey's anger.

Not more than a few days after this, something happened that was to determine the course of events to follow. For in the middle of the night, the glass of the door to the balcony outside the room where Hassaan slept was shattered. The serving girl who slept in the room with him screamed and called out for help. Safiyya, the bey, and the servants all came running. They peered down from the balcony and searched the garden, but there was no trace of the intruder.

My father said, in some confusion and without much hope, that glass sometimes shatters of its own accord, without anyone's having touched it. But how could he convince the bey it was not Harbi who had smashed the glass? How could he convince him that it was not Harbi who had tried to shatter the bey's joy in his son, the apple of his eye? Once the idea had entered the bey's mind, it took root there: he was convinced that Harbi wanted to kill Hassaan, so that the child would not inherit the bey's land and his estate. And who could hope to drive out an idea that had got into the consul's head?

After that, everything changed. The palace became like an armed fortress, surrounded by men with rifles, whose numbers were concentrated around the gate and in the corners of the gardens. The worst of it was that these men were not from our village. They were brutish Bedouins who respected no one, so that everyone entering the palace or leaving it was subjected to harassment and abuse. Not even women were spared. The consul-bey made no apology for this. His whole manner had changed a great deal, and he was no longer the man we remembered from before. He made no apology for the behavior of his men. As a result, my father put a stop to my mother's visits to Safiyya, and he himself seldom went to Luxor and the palace.

At that point, contact between our family and the bey's was mainly confined to Safiyya's occasional trips by car to visit us on her own. She would arrive laughing and radiant, and she would kiss my mother and sisters . . . but things were not as they had been. No more would my mother clap Safiyya on the shoulder, teasing her and saying, "What a disappointment you are, Safiyya!" She no longer made a fuss over her, and when my sisters saw her treating Safiyya with reserve and respect, they too quit joking with her as they had done before, except for little Abla, who was only four at that time. Her playfulness and the way she hung on Safiyya's neck seemed strange in that somber atmosphere. I scolded her and pushed her aside, but Aunt Safiyya protested, saying, "Why do you do that? Leave her be . . .

Abla is my darling, and I'm going to marry her to Hassaan." Then, as if that thought had reminded her of something, she said, "Oh . . . I've left Hassaan alone, and the bey will be home soon. I've got to get back to Luxor." My mother would urge her to stay for lunch, would insist that she stay, while Safiyya kept repeating that she must be on her way.

But, as my father said, if only the whole thing could have stopped there. And if only my mother had not asked me, that day, to bring lunch to Harbi at his house next to the fields.

Though many years have passed since that day, I remember it as if it were yesterday. I remember that it was a beautiful winter day, warm and sunny. It was like fall, when the sun's blazing heat lets up and a pleasant breeze blows, carrying no dust and no sign of a storm. It was a beautiful day also because the lentil plants, whose short green stalks covered the fields all along the road, had blossomed yellow overnight. They brightened the earth with their little yellow faces—a golden sea that rippled gently in the breeze, wafting their fresh, mild fragrance. All my life I have loved this scent and have never forgotten it, though those days are long gone.

So why did it all have to happen on such a lovely, pleasant day?

Harbi had asked my mother, who was like a sister to him, to prepare a milk pastry for him. She had done this, and she sent along a bit of lunch as well. He and I sat down to eat it in front of his house, which was right beside the fields, near the shade of a tall date palm. In the midst of this peace, we saw from far away the bey's car, the big red Ford, slowly approaching on the distant road. It gleamed in the sun, and Harbi could see it just as well as I could, but he bent his head over his food, and said nothing.

Only the two ruddy spots in his cheeks flushed more deeply, and his eyes grew dark with sadness. Then we heard the rattle and hum of the car as it approached the edge of the fields. I felt uneasy when I saw the car door open and the bey's body-guards—those strangers, with their rifles in hand—get out. Then the bey got out of the car. He was wearing a full suit and tarbush, as usual, and he carried a cane whose head was of ivory inlaid with gold. He approached the field where we were sitting, his men all around him. They didn't walk on the strip of land that ran beside the canal; rather they plunged into the midst of the crops, trampling them underfoot. Harbi stopped eating and got up. He stood tall and proud. "Welcome, Uncle," he said. The bey didn't answer but came toward me where I stood, next to Harbi. He put his hand on my head and asked me with a smile, "How are your mother and father? Go and tell them to prepare tea for me and my men." But for the first time I was afraid of him, afraid of his smile, and of his false teeth gleaming in the middle of his brown face. I moved away from the bey, and stood closer to Harbi, almost clinging to him as I heard him say once again, "Welcome, Uncle. You have honored your village and your land with your presence." But before we knew it, Harbi and I, the bey had reached out all at once and struck Harbi's cheek with a blow that caused the bey's tarbush and his entire, aging body to shake. His voice cracked as he shouted at Harbi in a tone I had never heard from him, "You dare to use that smooth tongue of yours with me, you dog?" The bey's feeble hand was not strong enough even to move Harbi's head, but I felt his whole body grow tense and ready, as if he were about to spring forward with all the strength of that body, and knock the bey to the ground. But instead he hung his head, and all the blood drained from his face. "Forgive me, ya bey," he said. "I'm your son and your servant. If I've done anything wrong, it's your right to punish me. Kill me if you wish. I wouldn't hurt the man who has been like a father to me."

I don't think that Harbi, as he spoke these words, had seen the four rifles that were pointed at him, or that he saw anyone or anything except the consul, his "father," whom he kept trying, until the very end, to convince of his innocence, and whose approval he was determined to regain. And I don't think that the bey—who after striking Harbi remained standing there, shaking with anger, his eyes red rimmed—had heard a thing his nephew said. But he heard me when I said, begging him, almost crying, "Please, ya bey, please don't hurt Harbi!"

The bey looked at me with his red-rimmed eyes, as if he were seeing me for the first time, and had never known me in his life. He pointed to me and said to his men, "Get the boy out of here." So one of them dragged me aside, then drew back and punched me with the force of his arm's full length, a hard blow to the chest. I fell down on the ground, with the wind knocked out of me. Every time I tried to catch my breath, I felt as though thorns were piercing my chest and my heart would burst. I stayed there in my place, sprawled on the ground and unable to get up, barely able to breathe at all. Nevertheless, I opened my eyes wide, not wanting to miss any of what was happening. I saw Harbi about to attack the man who had knocked me down, but at the same moment, the bey said to his men, pointing with his cane toward Harbi, "Strip this dog." Terrified, I continued to follow Harbi with my eyes as he struggled with the four men who were stripping him of his gallabiyya, vest, and undershirt, until nothing was left but his long underpants.

He was hitting them, and they were hitting him back. In the midst of the fight, he was shouting, "Please, Uncle! Kill me by your own hand . . . don't let these strangers do this to me, my father! Don't make me bear this shame, my grandfather! Kill me yourself!"

The bey was not listening, nor did he look at me or at anything else. He had taken off his tarbush and was drying the sweat on his brow while those men were stripping Harbi of his clothes. When they had finished and Harbi stood before the consul—his face, chest, and long underpants spattered with blood, his face and eyes swollen—the bey said calmly, "Don't be afraid, Harbi, and don't be in such a hurry to die. I'll make you wish for death, but you won't die."

Some farmworkers appeared at the edges of the field. They stood frozen when they saw the bey. One of them ventured to step forward, toward the bey, and they saw one of the gang of strangers aim his gun at them. But the bey reached out and lowered the muzzle of the rifle. Then he did no more than turn his head toward the men standing there watching and say, "I don't want anyone to remain here." He pointed his cane at Harbi, whom three of the thugs were holding fast. "This dog," said the bey, "has bitten the hand that fed him. Now leave me to punish him."

One of the farmers said, "Let him kiss your hand and your feet, ya bey, and then forgive him. We all kiss your hand . . ." The bey, whom no one had ever heard raise his voice before, flew into a rage. "Get out of here, you dogs!" he shrieked. "All of you would attack my house as he did, if you could! All of you would kill my son if you could, and rob me of my estate while I'm still alive! Get out, you dogs!" The farmers were frightened as they stood there, seeing him shout and wave his cane at them. They drew back some distance. But one old man didn't hesitate to say, loud and clear, "That's just the way Asran's kin used to deal with the peasants in the old days. Leave them now. Let them tear each other limb from limb."

But the others didn't see things that way. When one of them noticed me sprawled on the ground, he was reminded of something. "Run," he said, "go get the boy's father . . . The hagg is the only one who can put a stop to this."

I was still paralyzed with pain and terror. I couldn't move from where I was, and I wished my father really would come, because he alone would have managed to put a stop to what was happening. I heard Harbi, who was still bleeding from the nose, say in a broken voice, "How can I look anyone in the eye here in the village after this day, my uncle? How can you have wanted to shame your nephew this way . . . why didn't you kill me outright instead?"

The bey turned to him and said, "If this is all that's bothering you, Harbi, why then I'll put out your eyes, so that you can't see." Then he gestured toward his men, who dragged Harbi over to the palm tree. One of them took a long, coiled rope out of his pocket, and began to tie him up. By this time, Harbi had completely given up fighting them: it was all over as soon as the gang of outsiders had succeeded in stripping him of his clothes in public. His hands hung limp . . . his whole body went slack, and he let them do with him as they wished. Only he kept shaking his head, murmuring as if he were talking to himself, "Is this right, Uncle? Is this right, my father?" Meanwhile, the bey was keeping an eye on his men, and his whole face was drenched with sweat. He said to the men, "Just as I explained to you. You and you—tie him to the tree at the chest and legs, but leave a space between him and the trunk."

Two of the men held onto Harbi, bound hand and foot, while the other two began tying him to the trunk of the palm tree, wrapping one rope around his chest and the other around his legs, as the bey had ordered them to do. And Harbi allowed them to do all this to him, as if he were no more than a corpse. The bey walked over to him. He had taken hold of his cane, and prodding Harbi in the chest with it, he said, "You want me to kill you, Harbi? You want them to consider you a murder victim, and me to have to answer to them for the sake of a miserable parasite like you? What would you say, Harbi, if I made you wish for death without being able to die? Now, Harbi, you'll kiss my hand and beg me to kill you . . . but I won't give you the satisfaction of dying."

The bey gestured toward his men again, and two of them, one on either side, began to pull on the rope that bound Harbi by the chest, which was not quite taut. They lifted him up slowly, then set him down on the ground again. At first, Harbi didn't scream, even as the rough bark of the tree cut into his skin, ripping the flesh of his back and legs, but he cried words that rang with all the anguish of his soul, "Why, my uncle? Why all this . . . why?"

His uncle paid no attention, but kept right on prodding Harbi in the chest, laughing. "What do you say now, Harbi?" he said. "What say you leave this province and don't let me or anyone else see your face ever again till the day you die, far away from me and my son? What do you say, Harbi? I have an even better idea. Why don't you kill yourself with your own hand, and give yourself and me a rest? What do you say, Harbi?"

Harbi had begun to groan, opening his mouth wide, while they twisted him around the trunk of the tree, to the right, to the left, up and down. The blood had begun to flow from both sides, and from his shoulders, and he cried out more loudly now, with just two words, "Enough, Uncle! Enough!"

One of the Bedouin spoke up, warning him, "Ya bey, the skin's gone off his back, and we're down to the flesh now. You told us he wasn't to die. Our agreement didn't include murder."

The bey paid no attention. But Harbi, whose skin had been stripped away, and whose blood was now flowing from every part of his back, legs, and arms, gave one great cry as he flung himself forward, his pain alone giving him the strength to do so. The tall palm tree shook with the violence of his movement, and the ropes that had bound him broke. The ropes that had been tied around his chest were also torn free with the thrust, as he screamed the word, "Enough!" Quick as lightning, he bent down, untied his feet, and seized one of the men's rifles that was lying on the ground. With it he prodded the bey in the chest, still shouting, "Enough!" I cried out, too, when I saw his bloodied back, from which the flesh hung in strips. The bey yelled at his men, "Shoot! Are you men or women?"

But the leader of them said, "Our agreement didn't include murder, ya bey. We made a deal, and we're sticking to it, ya bey." Then the men turned and ran toward the car. They abandoned the bey, who stumbled as he backed away from Harbi, who was pushing him, the muzzle of the gun pressed to his chest. Harbi kept on shouting, "Enough! E-NOOOOOUUUUGH!" until finally he fired one shot into the bey's heart. The bey stood swaying a moment, his eyes bulging. "Oh," he gasped, "no . . . ," and with that he collapsed, landing facedown in the field of lentils.

From a distance I saw my father coming at a run, shouting "Stop, Harbi! Stop, ya bey! Harbi, stop . . ." The mayor was running behind him, and after him the village head watchman. The bey's men had reached the car, had started it, and were driving off in it. Harbi was gathering up his clothes, the blood still flowing from his body. With the rifle in his hand, he began running in the direction of the mountain. The bey lay stretched out on the ground in his black suit, amidst the yellow flowers.

My father stopped, and stared in horror at the scene before him. He didn't even see me. I don't know why, but he bent down and lifted up the bey's tarbush, which had rolled away into the flowers. He stood brushing it off and wiping it with the sleeve of his gallabiyya, saying over and over, "There is no strength or power, except in God."

It was the mayor, Hamid Asran, who knelt down and closed the bey's staring eyes. Then he stood up. He struck his palms together again and again in despair, repeating, "This is the ruin of our village."

It wasn't the ruin of the village, though, but of Harbi, whom I saw running, with a limping gait, his upper body bent over in pain. He began to stagger, as he shouted over and over that one word, "Enough! . . . Enough!"

It was my father who eventually rescued Harbi. He came across him, close to nightfall, lying facedown in the yellow sand.

"I found him," my father said, "still clutching the rifle. His back looked like some black waterskin, with the blood congealing on it. Harbi was still unconscious when I picked him up in my arms and carried him home."

And so my father brought Harbi, more dead than alive, to the hospital in Luxor. He waited until he regained consciousness, then persuaded him to report what had happened to the police and to turn himself in.

This is how Harbi's papers went north, to Asyut, and afterward to Cairo. For the case was tried first in the criminal court at Asyut. Then it was appealed in Cairo.

In Asyut, Harbi was sentenced to prison, at first for fifteen years at hard labor. Then, in Cairo, his lawyer convinced the court that Harbi had acted in self-defense. The testimony of prominent doctors was presented to show that what had happened there by the palm tree could well have been the end of him. After reviewing the case, the court commuted his sentence to ten years at hard labor.

When Aunt Safiyya heard that Harbi's sentence had been commuted, she said, "What of it? I wish they'd release him tomorrow. I want him here, in front of me. I want Hassaan to get a good look at the man he's going to kill when he grows up."

The villagers heard this and were silent. Even my parents and I said nothing.

How can I describe what happened to Safiyya after the bey was killed? I didn't see how she received the news; I was sick for a long time after that Bedouin's blow to my chest. Nothing I ate stayed down. My father brought a doctor to the house, who prescribed medication, but this didn't stop the vomiting; neither did it stop the screaming fits that seized me at night. These drove my mother, who sat up nights with me, into hysterics. She wept and struck her face with her hands, wailing as if a loved one had died, convinced that I was seeing the Angel of Death calling me. My father was forced to carry her bodily from the room, shouting at her, "He'll be just fine if you don't kill him yourself by carrying on like this!"

But I am not important to this story. What matters is what happened to my aunt Safiyya. I heard that she didn't cry or wail when they brought her the news. It was said that she hugged Hassaan to her and didn't speak for a while, until finally she said, "Too bad for you, Safiyya—your mother, your father, your husband, your son . . ." Then she kissed Hassaan, saying, "It's our fate, my child." It was said that afterward she stood up and went around to all the rooms of the palace, one after another. She gazed into each one then left it as it was, locking every door behind her. She ordered the servants to leave the palace, all of them, and not to lay a hand on anything or change even the position of a single chair . . . that was all. She asked them to take any food that was in the house, and go. Then she took the long black peasant robe that covers the body from head to foot, and she put it on over her store-bought dress. She took up Hassaan in her arms and told the driver to take her to the village.

She stopped first at the mayor's house, where the bey's body had been taken, and where the police chief and the district commissioner had gone. She didn't get out of the car. The mayor went and spoke to her through the car window. "My dear girl," he said, "you have my deepest sympathy . . ." Safiyya interrupted him. "I won't hear any such talk, ya ʿomda,"* she said. "I came

*Village elder—loosely, "mayor" (as it is translated elsewhere in the text).

to tell you one thing: bury your cousin as you think best, but accept no condolences. Tell everyone there is to be no funeral, and no mourning. There will be a funeral at the palace on the day when Hassaan avenges his father's death.* And on no account are you to tell anyone who killed the bey. Do you understand me, ya ʿomda?"

The mayor did not answer her: there was the district commissioner asking questions about the murderer, and here was Safiyya telling him not to say anything.

But Safiyya did not wait for an answer. She had already waved the driver on, and from there she went to the big house in the village, the house where the bey had so seldom stayed. It was like the rest of our houses, except that it had a mud-brick wall and it contained precious objects unknown in our houses.

I was astonished by the change that came over Safiyya after the bey was killed and she came back to live in the village.

I'm not talking about the fact that she stopped wearing the dresses she had worn at the palace and began wearing, like the rest of our women, the long, black jilbaab with the peasant robe over it, any time she went out. This was natural, since she was in mourning, and since she had decided to live in the village. What I'm talking about, rather, is a complete physical transformation. Within one month, my beautiful aunt Safiyya, who was not yet twenty years old, became an old woman. She even behaved the

*According to the conventions of vendetta and blood feud as traditionally practiced in Upper Egypt, the deceased is not formally mourned until his next of kin avenges his death by doing away with his killer. Thus it falls to Hassaan to act as Harbi's executioner, and the rites of mourning for the bey are to be postponed until he does so.

way old women do—or rather, she was allowed to behave like an old woman.

I know no explanation for what happened. But lines, like wrinkles, began to appear on her face and neck. She no longer wore only the jilbaab and the veil when she was at home, but took to wrapping a wide black kerchief around her neck as well. Her body, which had filled out a bit after the birth of Hassaan, grew thinner than it had ever been. Her soft skin began to roughen, and it grew browner day by day. Would it be improper for me to pass on what I heard my mother say to my sisters, namely that Safiyya, after she returned to the village, no longer took baths as often as she had when she lived in the palace, where she had been in the habit of bathing twice a day? I don't know whether that was due to sadness, depression, or laziness, but there was something—or so it seemed to me—that began to happen to her along with the darkening of her skin. It seemed to me that she began gradually to resemble the bey more and more, and that she came to sound more like him when she talked. She always spoke of him in the present tense, as if he had not been killed, had never been taken from her.

When she scolded the house servants, she would say, "This mess will annoy the bey." Or, "What will the bey say if he sees this?" Or, "The bey prefers to plant sugarcane in the eastern plot." And so on. She would say these things calmly and confidently, so that a stranger might think she was talking about someone who was just in the next room. By the time a few months had passed, there was nothing left of the Aunt Safiyya I had known, except for her green-gold eyes. And even those eyes, there in her brown face, had taken on a frightening intensity, a hardness that struck you when she looked at you. I saw children, the moment her glance fell on them, cry and clutch their mothers' sleeves. The children became still more frightened at the legends that grew up around her. For she would sometimes say things no one expected to hear.

I saw her once, a few weeks after the bey's death, when she first came back to live in the village, look into the eyes of a woman who was visiting her that day with some others. "Since when have you been pregnant, girl?" Safiyya asked the woman. The woman hid her face in her veil, embarrassed. "If only I were, Aunt Safiyya," she said, "but I had my period less than a week ago." But Aunt Safiyya said decisively, "You're pregnant." Less than a month later, the woman was telling this story in all the houses of the village, saying that Aunt Safiyya had known of her pregnancy before she herself was aware of it. A little while after that, Aunt Safiyya was making an agreement with one of the farmers concerning the planting of a certain piece of land. She said to him, "Beware of the snake that lives near this plot. If you kill him, don't leave his mate alive, for she will seek you out and kill you, even if you cross the seven seas to escape her." Afterward, when the man saw the big black snake creeping toward him as he worked hoeing the earth, he cut off the snake's head with his hoe. He didn't rest until he had searched all through the stalks of hemp that stood in a clump nearby, where he found the female snake guarding her eggs. He killed her and destroyed her eggs.

And yet, there was nothing out of the ordinary in all these things that Safiyya said. There were other women who could tell by intuition alone that a woman was pregnant. They could even determine the sex of the fetus, and their predictions would be right. And the eastern field was next to a jungle of hemp, in which snakes lurked. So Aunt Safiyya's warning was nothing unusual. Still, after these two incidents, it was widely believed in the village that Safiyya had second sight, and that the bey came to her nightly in her dreams to tell her what had been and what would be.

And so the beautiful Safiyya, whom all the men had desired, became the Aunt Safiyya whom all feared. She was granted the privilege of behaving in ways no one in the village did, except the old women. She would receive men in her home. And she farmed the land herself, in the sense that it was she who rented out the land to the farmworkers and received their payments. More than that, she determined what they should plant in each field—and this was a privilege not granted even to the old women among us who owned land. Normally, a woman would turn over the management of her estate to an uncle or a brother, and as a rule he would then take everything for himself, giving the woman just barely enough of the earnings to keep herself fed and clothed. This was not how it was with my aunt Safiyya, who took charge of the planting and leasing of land herself. She would go over the accounts with the shopworkers in Luxor, and with the real estate agents in Qena and Cairo. The only person she trusted, and to whom she delegated some of her work, was a merchant from Luxor who had been an old friend of the bey's. And the only thing she allowed him to do was to supervise the passage of the boats to the Sudan and the transport of goods. Had she been able, she would have done even this on her own.

The penniless men in the village, of whom there were a great many, looked on in amazement. They wondered what she was going to do with all the wealth she was amassing in the banks and the safes, in addition to what she had inherited from the bey. "What's she going to do with all that," they asked, "when she never goes anywhere, and she's such a skinflint?" My aunt Safiyya, however, wouldn't listen to any criticism or accept any teasing on this point. She spoke in the bey's quiet voice, but with conviction, saying, "No one is going to rob Hassaan of what's his. Hassaan's money is for Hassaan."

At that time, another businesswoman was also seen in our village, though she differed in her methods and manner. This was none other than Amuna el-Baida. All the men had thought they would have a better chance with her, after Harbi's imprisonment. But she gave up dancing at weddings and celebrations, and began to do as the other gypsies did: she carried a bundle of fabrics and a box of cheap wares, going from house to house, village to village with these things. She also told fortunes by drawing lines in the sand and casting seashells. There was no talk of her ever once having taken another lover after Harbi. As time went on, we saw less and less of her in the village. It was said that she was afraid of Safiyya. This surprised us, because the gypsy women were not usually afraid of anyone; rather it was they who made people afraid of them. Thus everyone became still more frightened of Safiyya.

At wakes, too, my aunt Safiyya started behaving as the old women did. Among our people, the women's mourning rites were not all sadness and grief. The actual mourning and wailing and reciting of eulogies went on for the first few days. After that, though, and throughout the remaining forty days, the wake would turn into a peaceful session that went on all day and included all the female relatives of the dead person—in other words, all the women of the village. Food would be brought every day from one or more of the houses, and the women would compare one woman's cooking to another's. After lunch, a fire would be lit and the gouza prepared. This was an innocent gouza, whose bowl—unlike that of the men's gouza—never held anything but honeyed tobacco. Then the pipe would go round the circle of old women. They might deign to give a puff to a woman who had been married for a long time. After all this, possibly following a short siesta, one of the women might begin the required rituals. Drawing out the word, she would say, "Oh, beloved!" At this point the wailing and eulogizing would begin, in loud voices, but after a little while the sobbing and weeping would subside again. Then the gouza would make the rounds again, with one woman saying to another, "That's enough, sister—you'll kill yourself! That will never do . . ." "Oh, if only I had died in his place (or her place) . . ." "Would you oppose the will of the Lord?" "God forbid! . . . and yet this is torment!" "May God relieve your suffering . . . here, sister, take the pipe . . . take a pull and calm yourself a little." This would go on until just before sunset. With each mourning period lasting forty days, the women were busy practically the whole year through, going from one wake to the next.

Although the gouza was normally forbidden to girls and young women, my aunt Safiyya had claimed the privilege of smoking it from the very first day she attended a wake after the death of the bey. She used to draw a long breath on the pipe and hold it as would someone who had been addicted for years, then exhale in stages through her nose, one puff after another, in a series of little smoke rings. I didn't like the women who smoked the gouza, but I continued to love Aunt Safiyya.

I was sad when my father quarreled with her for the first time. After the death of the bey, Safiyya retained her respect for my father, continuing to regard him as her father. She would kiss his hand when he arrived at her house, and would put the gouza away before he came in. None of this had changed, even though Safiyya knew that it was he who had saved Harbi's life, and who had retained the lawyers on his behalf in Asyut and Cairo. She knew, too, that he went once a month to Cairo to visit Harbi in prison. She understood that this was his duty. For his part, my father did not argue with her about her refusal to hold a funeral for the bey, or about her talk of Hassaan's avenging his father's death. Each understood that the other was doing what was expected.

But my father flew into a rage when he heard that Safiyya had given to a donkey—one that was used for manuring the fields—the name "Harbi." She had ordered the servant who tended its pen to bring "Harbi" to the courtyard of her house, where she would beat the animal with a cane, then instruct Hassaan, who was still no more than a baby, to spit on "Harbi." In this way, Hassaan learned to spit before he learned to talk.

I was with my father the day he went to see her. When he entered the house, and she was about to kiss his hand, he pulled it roughly away from her. "I'm angry with you, Safiyya!" he told her. "By my soul I'm angry with you!" She remained standing before him with her head down, but after a moment she looked up at him. She struck her chest, her eyes blinded by the tears that had suddenly filled them. "This fire, my father," she said, "just let me quench this fire that burns in me!"

She didn't ask him why he was angry. She knew as well as he did.

He said to her, "Pray to our Lord for solace. But don't do what is forbidden."

The tears vanished from her eyes as suddenly as they had appeared. In their place was that frightening gleam. "Is it not my right," she protested, "to instruct my son? Shouldn't he know who killed his father—a saint among men—so he can avenge him?"

My father answered this question carefully. "It was a man who killed Hassaan's father," he told her calmly, "not a donkey."

As if she hadn't understood, she replied, "A man?"

Then my father got angry again. "A human being, Safiyya! A human being, honored by God. It's a sin to call a donkey by a man's name! It's a sin! Do you understand?"

Safiyya let out a shrill cry. Her whole body twitched, and she began to beat her breast over and over, crying, "What about my revenge, ya hagg? What about this fire that consumes me?"

"I didn't say anything about your revenge, Safiyya," my father answered. "I said . . ."

But Safiyya wasn't listening. She was turning circles there in the broad courtyard, in the burning sun, striking her cheeks and tearing her hair. One of the servants was standing nearby, holding Hassaan, who began to cry when he saw his mother shouting and carrying on. But Safiyya paid no attention to him. She was moaning, a singsong wail, as she danced her crazy dance. "Harbi is my donkey," she chanted, "Harbi is my donkey. And the hagg wants to rob me of my revenge. Are you content with this, ya bey? Are you content with this, ya bey?"

She was staring at the sky, talking to the bey, whom she alone could see. My father grabbed my hand. He, too, was angry as I had never before seen him. "By God, ya Safiyya," he said, "if you don't stop what you're doing, I'll never set foot in your house again. For shame! A human being is no donkey!"

But to whom was he speaking? Safiyya continued to rave, turning in circles. A river of sweat poured off her, but still she wouldn't stop. My father pulled me away, almost dragging me, as he hurried out the door.

Once we were in the road, I could barely keep up with him. Feeling rather confused, I asked him how he could agree with Safiyya's plan for vengeance, when he was always preaching in the mosque against the vendetta system and trying to reconcile the families among whom quarrels ran rampant. My father was still boiling with anger. "Shut up, boy," he snapped.

I held my tongue. But his pace slowed a little, and he put his hand on my shoulder. For a little while he said nothing. Then suddenly he laughed softly, saying, "If your son grows up . . ."

My father came to a halt there in the road. He bent over me and grasped both my shoulders. The anger in his eyes had been replaced by a look that was almost sad. "Listen, my boy," he said, "I have faith in you . . . I have faith in Hassaan, once he is educated . . . I have faith that the time will come, when you and he are both grown . . ."

He stood looking into my face for a long time, as if to ask me whether I had understood. Then he sighed, took my hand, and we started walking again.

Afterward, there was no need for my father to fulfill his oath or to cut himself off from Safiyya. For a few days later, the servant found the field donkey dead in its pen, lying on its side, its legs sticking up stiffly in the air. They said that it had died of poison. Suspicion did not fall on anyone in particular, as there were many who were angry on Harbi's behalf.

Safiyya no longer used a donkey to instruct Hassaan after that: she turned to other methods.

But still sometimes—though rarely—I would find Safiyya to be as she had been before. At such times the beautiful Safiyya, whom I had loved, returned. For instance, I remember one occasion, when Hassaan had grown up a bit (he must have been three or four years old), when I had started preparatory school and begun carrying the boxes of cookies to our relatives and to the monastery on my own. In the morning I was wearing a new gallabiyya, skullcap, and shoes. I may also have been wearing the suit I went to school in, freshly ironed by my mother. I went out after my father, staying one step behind him. He embraced everyone he met in the street and gave him the traditional holiday greeting. On this day he wasn't wearing his gallabiyya. Instead he wore a jubbah and caftan, which had been ironed at a presser's shop in Luxor specializing in men's garments. For the people had insisted that my father deliver the holiday sermon. On that day, everyone was ready to open his heart. I can almost hear him now, the way he spoke out in his strong, melodious voice. "The feast day," he said, "is not for those who wear new clothes. No, it is for those whose hearts are new. If you pluck the spite from your hearts, every day of your life will be a feast day." I can almost hear him—his voice growing fainter and starting to tremble—when he spoke of the Prophet, all blessings and peace be upon him. He recounted the Prophet's sufferings before and after the Hijra, his wars and wounds . . . and my father's voice grew soft and full of sadness. Then it picked up strength again, swelling with joy as he described how God had rewarded the Prophet, how He joined together hearts that had been at war. He stopped speaking for a few moments, passing his eyes over the group of worshipers. I can almost feel the way he wished to grasp each man by the shoulders and say to him, "I have faith!"

After prayers, I hurried back home. I received my mother's words of advice as to what I must do with the holiday gifts. She repeated to me a thousand times that I mustn't appear joyful when I took Safiyya's box to her. One minute she was pleading with me, the next she was threatening me with punishment if I should make a single mistake. So off I went to my aunt Safiyya's, pursued by those words of warning. I behaved with the sobriety of a man who goes to visit a woman who is in perpetual mourning. I put the box to one side, saying calmly, "My mother has sent this for Hassaan." I didn't bring up the subject of the feast day by mentioning the word "cookies."

But Aunt Safiyya had lightened her mood that morning, for Hassaan's sake. She hadn't taken off her mourning garb, but the black clothes she wore were new. She had washed and brushed her hair, and taken out the gouza, which she had not been allowed to smoke during the month of Ramadan. She had dressed Hassaan in a new outfit and seated him beside her. This and the box I had brought her were all the holiday there was for her. For no one visited her on that morning, and the servants were not allowed, while in the house, to behave as if it were a feast day. Even so, I was glad for this slight change, for I found my aunt Safiyya as she had been when I grew up loving her. She put aside the gouza when she saw me, and greeted me with outstretched arms. "May all of you be always well,"* she said. Remembering my mother, I didn't dare answer her in kind. "And Hassaan, too," I stammered. I went over to Hassaan and picked him up and kissed him. "Hasn't Hassaan grown?" she said anxiously. "Just look how he's grown!" *"Bismillaahi maa shaa' allah,"* I replied. "He's grown a lot. He's become a man!" She reached out and took him from me. Hugging and kissing him, she said, "I can't wait to see him become a man like you! If only I could close my eyes, and find when I opened them that he had become a man . . ." "God give you long life, Aunt Safiyya," I said to her. "May the Lord hear you," she said firmly. "I want to live long enough to see his father rest in peace." She got up then, carrying Hassaan. In the room was a glass cabinet. She went over to it and unlocked it with a small key which she took from her pocket. In the cabinet was a box inlaid with seashells and a red velvet case, which held the bey's medal. The medal always shone, because Aunt Safiyya polished it every day. She opened the box and took out a new pound note, which she handed to me, saying simply, "The bey has sent you this holiday present." I tried hard to refuse, as my parents had told me to do, but Safiyya pressed the pound note against my chest. "For heaven's sake take it," she said. "Don't upset the bey."

And so, with a mixture of pleasure and embarrassment, I took it, since Safiyya was no longer intimately connected to me, no longer a member of my family as she had been before. Then she busied herself with a conversation that was forever being repeated between her and Hassaan. Pointing at the medal, she

*Traditional holiday greeting, to which the standard reply is "And you also."

said, "Look, Hassaan, your father is a king! What is your father?" "My father is a king," answered Hassaan. He must have reached out for the medal then, but she gently moved it out of his reach. "I want to play with the king!" he said to her. She replied laughing, "When you grow up and become worthy of the king." Hassaan started to cry, and Safiyya tried to distract him.

I felt frightened for the little boy, when I saw how she played with him, and he was scared, too. She was tickling him vigorously and babbling at him, "Du-du, du-du-du, Hassaan-bey is a bey, Hassaan-bey, Hassaan-bey . . . When they told me 'It's a boy!' I held my head high with pride . . . du-du, du-du-du, du . . ." At first Hassaan laughed when she tickled him; then he began to cry, "No, Mommy, no, Mommy!" laughing because he couldn't help it, then by turns laughing and sobbing loudly. But now Safiyya had grown tired and dizzy. With all this frantic roughhousing, her breath had begun to come in short gasps. This was also on account of her addiction to the gouza. So she called one of the servants and handed over Hassaan, who seemed eager to get away from his mother. She sat down on the floor, which was spread with carpets. She leaned her back against the wall, and before she had even caught her breath, she had already taken out the gouza and was searching among the ashes in the little fireplace for burning embers. I saw her eyes gleaming green and gold, as she grasped the coal with the tongs and blew on it, before placing it in the bowl. She forgot about me for a little while, as she inhaled on the pipe. Her whole face had grown flushed, as she blew the little smoke rings from her nose, expelling them in rapid succession, and then coughing. After a little while, she opened her eyes, and looked at me absentmindedly. "Won't you stay and have lunch with your aunt Safiyya?" she asked me. But my mother had warned me not to delay, for there were other boxes I had to deliver. A steady look had returned to Safiyya's green-gold eyes.

How brief were the moments in which this Aunt Safiyya became once again *my* aunt Safiyya, whom I used to know and love.

CHAPTER THREE

The Outlaws

I was in my second year of high school, and examinations were coming up, when I noticed that my father had recently taken to visiting the monastery more often, without taking me along. One evening he came into my room while I was studying. Frowning, he said, "Leave whatever you're doing and come with me."

Puzzled, I followed my father to his room. I was trying to figure out what could be important enough to make him do such a thing, when he was the one who was forever urging me to study harder. I thought to myself it couldn't be about the marriage of Ward es-Sham. It was true that lately a certain young man, one of our relatives, had been spending more time with my father, and my mother whispered to me that she prayed to God he would propose to Ward es-Sham. This would open the way for her younger sisters, for they could not be married off before the oldest. But I told myself he wouldn't come and interrupt my studying for that, looking so troubled.

When we had gone into my father's room, he locked the door behind him. He seated himself on the prayer rug and gestured for me to sit down in front of him. He sat there silent for awhile, moving the beads of his misbaha in one hand, rubbing his forehead with the other. Then he made up his mind. Gathering up the prayer beads in his hand, he said to me in a whisper, "There's something I need to speak to you about."

I kept quiet, waiting for him to speak. After a moment he said, moving closer to me, while his voice grew even softer, "They're going to release Harbi."

Overjoyed, I exclaimed, "Harb- . . ."

But before I could get the name out my father had clapped his hand over my mouth. "Not one word," he said.

I understood, and was silent. My father said, "What do you think?"

I thought for a moment. Then I said, lowering my voice as he had, "There's still a lot of time before Hassaan grows up—and then the Lord will provide a solution." My father replied, with a sigh, "That is, if Safiyya waits until he grows up. I'm afraid she won't have the patience . . . in fact, I'm almost sure she won't have the patience."

An idea came to me. "What if we married him to Ward es-Sham?" I said.

I knew that Ward es-Sham's being still unmarried—and therefore likewise the other girls—cut my father deeply, just as it did my mother, only more so. He was afraid that the reason his daughters still had no suitors, with the oldest girl nearly twenty, was his insistence on giving them an education. Of all the girls in the village who were about Ward es-Sham's age, she was the only one who had completed preparatory school, and the only one still unmarried. Although we didn't discuss this subject, I could tell that my father sometimes blamed himself for not having followed village custom. He was afraid he might have ruined his daughters' chances for the future. So I thought that my idea would kill two birds with one stone, but my father, trying to hide his smile, said, "My, what a clever idea!" I faltered and said no more, overcome with embarrassment. From the way he had spoken, it was clear he thought I was completely off the mark. He kept silent, waiting for me to say something. Without much conviction, I said, "I figured, since Safiyya loves Ward es-Sham as a sister, she might think twice before killing her sister's husband."

With a sigh of resignation and a wave of his hands, my father replied, "I thought you were smarter than that."

Then he leaned forward, pointed at his heart, and said, "You can be sure that Safiyya wouldn't hesitate to kill even me, who raised her, and who's like a father to her, if I stood between her and her revenge."

"Then he should stay in Cairo," I said.

"And who'll look after him there? And who can guarantee that she wouldn't find out where he was? The bey's friends and henchmen are everywhere in Egypt." My father bowed his head. "Harbi is ill," he said sadly. "They're releasing him from prison before his sentence is up, because he's in such bad health."

I kept silent. At that moment I was also overcome with grief and anxiety. I sat gazing at my father, trying to read his thoughts. He didn't keep me wondering long, but spoke right up, though without raising his voice. "Listen," he said, "I've thought of everything. Tomorrow morning, hook up the carriage. You and I will go to the station at dawn, before anyone knows about it."

I said in surprise, "We're going to Cairo?"

He shook his head. "No," he replied, "we're going to meet Harbi at the train that comes from Cairo. We'll take him to the monastery. I asked Brother Girgis to request permission from the head of the monastery, and he agreed that Harbi could stay there. He can live on the monastery farm. Safiyya won't be able to harm him while he's under the protection of the monastery. No one will be able to lay a hand on him."

I hesitated. "The monastery?" I said. "But . . ." My father raised his hand in front of my face, saying in the same tone, as if he hadn't heard me, "And from now until morning, I don't want anyone in the house to hear a thing about this. The whole village will know soon enough, but for now I want not a word. Not even a bird in the sky must know, or else they might kill him before he gets off the train."

And so we went out at dawn. The village was used to my father's going to Cairo sometimes on the train that left at dawn, so none of our neighbors was surprised to hear the noise of the horse and carriage in the dark of night. A few people who were leaving the village on that train were startled to see my father standing on the arrival platform, waiting for the train coming from Cairo. When the train pulled in, they saw him supporting a tall, hooded figure who was getting off. They saw my father lead him quickly out of the station. The carriage was parked right in front of the station door. Harbi got into the back seat, and my father, taking no chances, drew the carriage roof. Then he said to me, "Show us what you're made of. I want us to be in the village before a single person returns from the station."

My father gave the horse's neck a gentle pat, then climbed up next to Harbi. I sat alone on the raised front seat, silently praying to God not to let the old horse go slack on me on the way but to let him fly, as my father put it, "like a dove." Did the horse sense that secret prayer? Could he feel my uneasiness as I sat in the carriage, cracking the whip over his head without touching him, clutching the reins and shouting urgently at him to get going? Had my father's brief, gentle touch on his neck before he got into the carriage also been a secret message to our old brown horse not to delay us on that difficult morning? Was it our tension and anxiety that made him take to the road as if all the spirit and lightness of youth had suddenly come back to him, to the point where my father shouted at me from inside the swaying carriage to pull in the reins or we would all tumble over the embankment? I don't think my father could possibly have heard me, with all the din of our crashing into potholes and the squeaking of the wooden wheels—which I was afraid might fall apart—when I shouted back that I could barely control the reins, either to pull them in or let them out, that I was all but clinging to them for dear life. And what did the villagers think when we arrived in the village and all that noise brought them out of their houses? They saw me, alone, driving that carriage run amok, but they couldn't make out the two figures sitting inside. Some of them ran after me, yelling, "Stop, you lunatic! You'll destroy the carriage . . . you'll kill people's chickens! (The boy's lost his mind—his father will kill him!) We'll tell your father!" And what did they think when they saw me reach our house at last, not stopping there, but heading east, straight into the desert, while the horse kept on, through the sand and the pebbles in the middle of his path, avoiding rocks and holes, like he knew every stone, every ditch along the way, galloping along with the carriage in tow, on that rough road he'd never been on before, until finally I pulled up by the monastery gate. My father got out. Harbi got out. My father said laughing, almost in a whisper, "Were you trying to rescue Harbi or kill all three of us?" Then he grabbed my arm and added proudly, "God keep you, my boy." I was panting, the horse was panting. He lifted his head, his nostrils trembling, pulling in the air in quick breaths, while his black eyes rolled, their whites showing plainly. Then he bent his neck and leaned his head toward me questioningly. I said with a smile, "Come on, ya miqaddis Bishai . . . this horse also deserves some attention!"

And the miqaddis Bishai did come in fact. He opened the door and admitted my father and Harbi, saying formally, "Welcome, hagg and hagg." He didn't say Harbi's name. And he forgot about me, as he closed the door quickly behind him.

But we knew, my father, the old horse, and I, that we had succeeded: we had saved Harbi.

My father took care of the arrangements. He had a small hut built in the middle of the farm lands, well away from the monastery buildings and near the miqaddis Bishai's hut. He made Harbi swear that he wouldn't leave this farm for any reason whatsoever, though he said to him sadly, "I know that when you can't come and go as you like, that's a prison as well, but we have no choice. Be patient, son of my father. Remember our Lord, and pray to him, Harbi. Find pleasure in prayer so that the space of this little hut opens out before you and widens as if it were the whole earth . . . look upon Heaven before you enter it by the will of God."

Harbi listened and trusted my father's words. He'd learned a new way of speaking in Cairo, and so he replied, "Certainly, sir." Then he caught himself, shook his head as if to clear it, and said, "Right, son of my father . . . what you're saying is right . . . God have mercy on me."

It was all I could do to keep from crying out when I saw Harbi after he pulled the hood back from his face. He had lost most of his hair, and his cheeks had become two blue smudges, scattered with small scars and wounds. In his eyes was the look of a light that had gone out—his whole face was like a lamp that had been put out.

On the way home from the monastery, I tried unsuccessfully to find out something from my father about Harbi's illness—he kept sighing and saying, "Just pray that he'll get well . . . God's mercy is great."

Contrary to what I expected, the village did not object to the arrangements my father had made. There were two or three people who were unhappy with what he had done, and who openly criticized him after Friday prayers in the mosque. My father listened to them in silence. Then he spoke slowly, in the presence of the whole crowd, saying, "Did not our Beloved Prophet, blessings and peace be upon him, send the first Muslims to el-Nigashi, in defense of their lives? I take solace in the Beloved, the Chosen One." The crowd responded, "Amen!" and after that no one said a word; Harbi was well loved in the village, and from that point on, the number of his visitors at the farm grew. As for Aunt Safiyya, she did not set foot in our house after that day. My father didn't go to see her, but my mother visited her one time because he asked her to, and she returned grim faced. She announced the moment she walked in the door—and this was the first time I ever heard her raise her voice to my father—"You've disgraced me, ya hagg! No less than drive me away, that's what she did! You know the hell Safiyya is living, so why did you make me go to her? We deprive her of her revenge, then we go and rub her face in it? My God, this is unspeakable!"

But my father waved his hand, saying, "I've done as my Lord would have me do, and that's good enough. Leave the rest to God."

This wasn't the first time I realized that my mother was on Safiyya's side, despite her affection for Harbi—whom she, too, used to call "son of my father"—and despite the fact that she knew he had suffered the injustice of el-Hasan and el-Hussein. Something deeper than all of that kept reminding her that Safiyya would never rest until she took her revenge, and she was convinced that this revenge was Safiyya's right.

Sometimes I would find her alone, weeping, crouched on the ground, rocking back and forth and crying, "Poor Safiyya, my poor girl!" And sometimes she would turn toward me and say, as if still talking to herself, "The bey will be on your conscience forever, until Judgment Day, and he'll never rest in his sleep."

Nevertheless, all contact had been cut between Safiyya and our family. I no longer saw her, but I heard a lot about her. I heard that from the time Harbi had arrived, she had begun going round to people's houses. She would go from house to house all day long, saying, "Do you see? The bey was right. Do you see? He knew Harbi was no better than a woman. And here he is, just like a woman. Here he is, hiding from a woman and a child, under the protection of the Christians. If he's a man, then let him come out. Who's he afraid of? Who's he afraid of? Hassaan is a foot and a half tall. Is he afraid of Hassaan, or should I be afraid of him for Hassaan's sake? Tell him to come out! Ask this woman why he's afraid of a woman!"

The people listened but said nothing. A short time later, we were startled to learn that Safiyya had driven off the two armed guards who had stood in front of her house. The two men didn't explain the reason, but we heard that she had ordered them to go to Harbi at the monastery and kill him. The men said, "Madame Safiyya, if he comes out of the monastery, we'll kill him, but we can't kill him within the monastery grounds. Even criminals and outlaws don't do that—it's a sin!"

It was said that she was sitting on the ground when this took place and that she got up and threw the stove at them with its burning embers, shouting, "Get out of here, you women! Am I being guarded by females? Go and sleep next to him! Take your rifles, and take two of my dresses, you women . . . !"

It was said that the two men ran away, shaking off the embers from their clothes as they went, and it was said that she kept after them, running barefoot behind them, until the servants carried her into the house. It was said that she had gone crazy, or was about to. But the farmers who rented land from her said that not a penny escaped her reckoning, that her mind was as sharp as any in the whole village.

This is what was said; I hadn't seen any of it. I didn't set eyes on her, that day or afterward, but I did see Harbi. In spite of everything, my mother continued to prepare for him the kind of food he liked, and I would bring it to him. Other relatives also went on visiting him and bringing him food. As a result, his hut was always heaped with these visitors' gifts, though Harbi had little appetite and didn't eat much. His neighbor, the miqaddis Bishai, joined him at meals and would usually press him to eat, although he was himself a more modest eater even than Harbi. The two of them would take their meals underneath the palm trees that stood between their two huts. They would sample bites of this and that, dipping it into whatever was at hand, and then they would lose themselves in conversation. Though I sometimes joined them, I was too shy to impose on them at meals; I always knew, in any case, that I would eat when I got home.

Their talk was in general much like that of the villagers in their nightly sessions. It had to do with our ancestors, who had built the village after their escape from the crown estates, and their descendants and how the passage of time had affected them. It also touched on how Asran's star had risen. Asran was the grandfather of the largest family in the village, and a few of his descendants were wealthy. Although the miqaddis Bishai—like all the monks in that monastery—was not originally from the village, all the same he had been a companion of the late Bakhoum and had heard many things from him. Later, the miqaddis Bishai was able to fill in the details through his frequent association with us.

Harbi would talk to him in all seriousness, despite the fact that the miqaddis Bishai often got things mixed up: as, for example, in his tale of how Asran achieved the rank of a bey. We—Asran's descendants—had heard that he obtained the bey rank after a visit to Luxor by the Khedive, to whom he had rendered various services. But the miqaddis Bishai said that Asran had achieved this status because he invited the Egyptian navy to a great banquet. Harbi laughed at this. "How," he asked, "did Asran invite the Egyptian navy to a banquet, ya migaddis? Did there use to be an ocean in our village that's since dried up?" The miqaddis Bishai insisted that he had heard this from the late Bakhoum, who had witnessed the event with his own eyes. He added that the tables Asran laid for the navy reached all the way from the village to the monastery. The members of the fleet had worn brocade, he said, and Asran had slaughtered all his livestock in order to feed them. He had brought two cooks and two waiters from Luxor—from the "Winter Palace," no less—and they wore brocade, too, he said. When his highness the King Abbas heard this, he sent Asran "a big gold bekawiya." With this gold, Asran bought a lot of land, which his children later inherited.

When the miqaddis Bishai found that Harbi was still laughing in spite of everything, and that I was trying to hide my grin, he tilted his head, squinting. With that air of embarrassment we knew so well, he said, "I mean, my boy, do you think the navy couldn't get here any other way than by sea? Couldn't they have come by train? Weren't they people just like the rest of us, even if they did wear brocade?"

Harbi, embarrassed in his turn, and ashamed of himself for laughing at the monk, replied, "Yes, you're right, ya migaddis."

But other kinds of conversations took place between Harbi and Bishai when they were by themselves. These were mostly on agricultural matters: what would improve the quality of the soil and what would not, what were the best months for planting this, the right times for watering that. Such discussions were no joking matter, for the two sometimes disagreed, raising their voices to such a pitch that a stranger might think they were on the point of a serious quarrel.

One day when Bishai was working in the field, I saw that Harbi had removed his gallabiyya and picked up a hoe in order to help him. When I mentioned this in passing to my father, his face changed color and he flew into a rage. He leaped to his feet. "Come with me," he ordered. The reason for his anger dawned on me, and I instantly regretted having spoken up, but it was too late for that. My father rode his white donkey, while I followed him on another mount. The whole way, he goaded and cursed at his donkey in a way that was not at all like his usual self.

It was just as well that the miqaddis Bishai was not there when we arrived. My father exploded at Harbi the moment he saw him, "Since when, Harbi, do you behave like tenant farmer, hoeing and ploughing?" Harbi tried to calm my father, at the same time looking accusingly at me. "It wasn't work, ya hagg," he said, "I was amusing myself." "You don't say?!" my father replied. "And were you amusing yourself all those years ago by hoeing your own soil? Have you ever heard of any man of standing in our village working the land like a tenant farmer? Are you trying to disgrace me, Harbi, in my old age? What would Safiyya say if she heard that you'd picked up a hoe and were working on the land at the monastery? She'd say they'd hired you. You're going to make yourself and me the laughing-stock of the village. Have you lost your mind, Harbi?"

Harbi hung his head. "Forgive me, son of my father," he said. "It happened once, it's over, and I won't let it happen again."

Harbi, like my father, was one of the leading figures in our village. The lowest work he could do was to guard his land by night with a rifle in his hand or to supervise the field hands and the tenant farmers, advising and directing them. He must not turn his hand to the actual labor of farming. None of the village elite was really wealthy, and none of them owned anything more than he needed, except for the consul-bey, of course, God rest his soul; still, boasting was one of the vices of the village. So at some of the gatherings where men got together to talk and joke, tongues were loosened as the hookah passed from hand to hand. Or, after a glass or two of ʿaraq (or "the date," as the villagers called it) in the back room of ʿAmm Rizq's grocery, someone would brag about the hundreds of pounds he had squandered during his last visit to Cairo, where he had been in the habit of staying up all night with some of his Cairene friends, among whom were officers of the revolutionary council. Or someone would claim that he had certain moneys owing to him from the bey's estate, but that he was reluctant to claim his due, as this might grieve Safiyya, and so he preferred to leave the matter to God's accounting. Or it might happen, as the evening wore on, that one member of the group would turn sorrowful, put his head in his hands, and moan that he didn't know how he was going to come up with the bribe money* for the outlaws, who had sent for him specifically, demanding such and such a sum. But everyone knew all this was nothing but fantasy that would vanish like smoke, and that each man had to humor his brother, because if a man missed his chance today to plead his case before the listeners, then he'd have another chance tomorrow.

*Money extorted by a mafia-like (though less elaborately organized) group, in exchange for which the group would refrain from harassing those who paid the bribe on demand.

And so we were very surprised when one day there appeared in our poor village an army of men dressed in black gallabiyyas and white turbans, with machine guns and rifles slung over their shoulders. We were even more surprised to see them pass through the village, then leave it behind and make for the monastery. I saw them. There were about twenty of them, who passed through the streets and alleyways of the village without turning to the left or to the right, and without speaking to anyone. Their leader was a terrifying giant of a man, who did not carry a rifle on his shoulder. Instead he held a long stick, which he grasped in the middle, striking the ground in front of him with it as he walked, reaching it out to arms' length at each step. His gallabiyya fit him tight across the chest and billowed around his feet, like a black sail leading that ill-omened band over the yellow sands. I didn't dare follow them, but some others who were not paralyzed with fear went sneaking along—at a safe distance—behind those outlaws who had never before set foot in our village and saw them stop some distance from the monastery door. They saw the leader of the band go up to the door and knock on it with his stick.

The miqaddis Bishai said later that he had never in his life known fear such as he felt when he opened the door and saw that face, and beyond it all those faces. He stood paralyzed, and the man spoke to him, but he didn't hear. And he still didn't understand anything when he saw the giant shout at his men to throw down their rifles and sit down on the sand. The only thing he got was that the man wanted Harbi. The miqaddis Bishai told us that at that moment the Age of Martyrs came to his mind, and he found the courage to say, "We won't give him up. We won't hand over our guest." He was about to close the door, but the giant lost his temper and put out his hand to keep the door from closing. "Believe me, my boy," said the miqaddis Bishai, "this was no arm—it was an iron rod that pushed the door aside and me with it, almost knocking me to the ground. He was shouting in my face, 'Listen!' And at that moment the Lord willed Brother Girgis to come." Brother Girgis was able to make some sense of the situation, but he asked the man to go around the monastery, to go unarmed, and to leave his men sitting in front of the monastery gate. It was said that Harbi, when he saw the giant approaching his hut, rushed toward him with his arms outstretched, crying, "Faris!" The giant, embracing Harbi, replied in a hoarse voice, "Your servant, oh master of men."

But this was the only time that a member of the band of outlaws entered the monastery grounds. The head of the monastery would not allow this scene to be repeated.

We knew part of Faris's story. We knew that he was the leader of the band of outlaws in our province and that his name alone struck fear in people's hearts. The previous leader, Ateito, had been an evil man. Not only had Ateito extorted bribes from the wealthy and the needy alike, but he had seized for his own use a large piece of land at the foot of the mountain to the north of the province. There he grew hashish and opium, which he then sold. Also he was an uncontrollable murderer. He would ambush people on the road, killing them with or without cause. But after he attacked some people who had prominent relatives in Cairo, the government took action. They sent in the army, which then besieged Ateito on the mountain. A war ensued in which for some time neither side gained the upper hand. For several weeks the newspapers kept reporting about the "pincers" that were closing in on the criminal and the noose that was being tightened around his neck. But Ateito didn't fall to any pincers. He was surrounded one night, in the middle of the night, in the house of a woman of leisure he used to frequent, at the foot of the mountain. He hadn't left off going to see her, even after the noose began to tighten around his neck.

The newspapers published a picture of him the next day. The bullets had pierced his chest, turning him into a sieve. His mouth was open and strangely twisted. For a long time after that, we continued to see articles about the purging of the mountains. Then the government bombarded the outlaws' strongholds with its planes and burned the opium and hashish farms.

When the outlaws came out of hiding again several months later, it was under a new leader: Faris. It was said that people's fear of them had dwindled after the killing of Ateito, to the point where one of the wholesale grocers in the capital of the province announced openly that he would not pay the bribe, and that Faris could "go drink river water."* Faris went by himself to see the man at high noon one day. When the merchant saw him coming like perdition itself, he spread his arms in welcome, saying, "Greetings to our miʿallim, crown of our head!" But Faris didn't answer. He entered the shop, grabbed the man by the hair, then smashed his head against the marble floor the way a ruffian might smash an onion with his fist. It was said that a single blow left him sprawled limp armed on the marble, blood pouring from his head onto the floor. Then Faris sat in a nearby

*Roughly equivalent to "go jump in the lake"; or, a bit stronger, "go to hell."

coffeehouse, calmly smoking the shisha for an hour or so during which no one dared enter the shop to see if the man was alive or dead. After that, people knew what Faris was capable of. But it was said of him that he would not extort bribes from a poor man or a woman, and that he offered protection at no cost to his neighbors at the foot of the mountain.

Harbi had known Faris in prison, before any of this happened. They were companions at hard labor in the Tura Penitentiary. They went out at dawn to the mountain where they worked quarrying stone, and each prisoner was assigned a daily quota he had to fulfill, before the men could return to their cells. The guard in charge of them accepted no excuses. He would whip any man who fell short of his quota, order him to be deprived of food, and make him stand naked in the sun for hours. And it was only with great difficulty that each prisoner was able to offer up his quota of stone at the end of the day. Faris, however, had no problem fulfilling his quota. His hand was, as Bishai said, a tool of iron, and he had never been sick a day in his life. But once he came down with something that affected only his eyes. The prison doctor gave him eyedrops and applied some ointment, but refused to exempt him from going to the quarry.

Faris, a real man, was not one to complain. Although he could barely see, he went to the quarry.

Harbi saw him fumbling with his pickaxe, striking now at the stone, now at the air, random blows that scattered the dust but didn't crack the stone. He went up to Faris and said to him, "Sit down, cousin. I'll be responsible for your quota and mine until God heals your eyes." At the end of the week, Harbi, who had been turning in two daily quotas of stone all week, could no longer stand on his two feet. Faris embraced him and told him,

"If ever you need these eyes of mine, cousin, I'll pluck them out for you."

So the outlaws began frequently to appear unannounced in our village—sometimes they came once a month, other times once a week. In the beginning, Faris wanted to take his friend with him and to see to his protection, but Harbi politely turned down this offer. Then the leader of the outlaws suggested to my father that he, Faris, should go himself to "the lady Safiyya," and offer her the blood price she demanded. But my father managed to talk him out of this plan, telling him it was useless, and that it would be better not to put himself in the way of refusal—or worse. My father foresaw what Faris's reaction would be to Safiyya's nervous behavior, and so by preventing their meeting he was taking care to protect her as well as Harbi.

The days the outlaws came to visit were the only days Harbi ever went outside the monastery. Brother Metri, the head of the monastery, was determined that they should stay outside the walls, and he scolded Bishai and Brother Girgis for having let Faris go into Harbi's hut the first time. He said with finality, "No one who lives outside the law shall enter the sanctuary of the monastery." Faris, not wanting to cause Harbi any problems, did not argue with this. But he always made sure he protected his friend whenever he left the safety of the monastery: the outlaws would stand guard with their rifles on the mountain lookouts around the monastery, and Faris would put his hand on Harbi's shoulder as soon as he came out, ready to defend him with his own body from any treachery. Then they would stretch out on the sand, surrounded by a circle of Faris's men.

During those visits, Faris and his men would behave like Arab sheikhs who followed the rules of proper behavior. They never arrived empty-handed. Rather, they came carrying gifts of fruit and pastry for Harbi. His hut was always piled high with such presents—brought also by his relatives in the village—which he would distribute to the monks. The outlaws would always treat my father with respect and would all stand up, with Faris at their head, whenever he appeared during one of their visits. They would lower their voices when they spoke, and leave off cursing. There were some Christians among Faris's men, who would press coins into the miqaddis Bishai's hand, and ask him to put these into the monastery's collection boxes and to light candles for them in the chapel.

Bishai was the only one of the monks who would join Harbi and the outlaws on the days of their visits. He got into the habit of bringing them tea from the monastery, and he would light a lantern for them if it got to be late at night and they were still sitting on the sand outside the walls.

The outlaws soon became fond of him, just as the villagers were fond of him. They took to joking with him and comfortably asking him to fix them another round of tea. He would do so without complaint. Bishai took to joining them in their late-night conversations, although one of the outlaws, a Christian whose name was Hinein, would sometimes go too far in teasing him. He would look very serious and ask the miqaddis Bishai about the secrets of the monastery and monasticism, saying that he was thinking also of becoming a monk. The miʿallim Faris responded to this more than once rather irritably, but Hinein said with exaggerated innocence, "Do you begrudge me some happiness ya miʿallim? Maybe I'll be ordained, and become like this good man." And Bishai would say, laughing his loud laugh, "Don't be ordained and don't become a monk, ya Hinein . . . but do give up bad company, and leave the path of evil so you can follow the way of our Savior."

Hinein replied in a voice of great longing, with his hand on his chest, "Anywhere you go, I'll be right beside you. Take me with you, and I'll follow the way . . ." It didn't make the miʿallim Faris angry when the miqaddis Bishai talked about the path of evil; rather he would laugh loudly in his turn, saying, "If only you really would take him with you, ya migaddis, and rid us of him. There's nothing to him but hot air and a headache!"

If Hinein kept up his teasing after that, the miʿallim Faris would turn a stern eye on him, and Hinein would cut short his talk, all but shrinking away under that angry glance.

Sometimes when the visit stretched into the night, and the lanterns were brought out to light up the mountain, the miʿallim Faris would ask Harbi to sing. He told us that when Harbi sang in prison, silence fell on the cells, and even the guards listened. Harbi would agree to his request, as we sat there on the sand. He would begin singing softly, with bowed head. Then, little by little, he would raise his voice until his sad song echoed off the mountain and rang through the air.

In those days, he would improvise to the night, to the long night, to the night whose stars clung by their roots to the sky. To the chains of silver that kept the darkness fettered in the sky, so that the stars would not move, and the night would remain unchanged. At that time, cries of longing would rise up from the throats of Faris and his men—cries that carried the weight of their buried cares and sorrows. And the tears would flow from my eyes when I thought of Harbi as he had once been—the Harbi of whom nothing remained but that beautiful voice and its improvisations that sang of sadness.

Those shadowy nights on the mountain, when Harbi's voice alone would hold our circle spellbound, spread out upon the sand—how well I remember them!

But, as our people would say, nothing—neither day nor night—stays the same. True enough, for I remember also that day when our troubles with the outlaws began.

One morning, an officer from Luxor came to our house, an unheard-of event until that day. This was a little while after the disastrous defeat of 1967, when an atmosphere of gloom had settled on our village, like everywhere else. We had seen the calamity with our own eyes, when the airplanes flew above our heads—those planes with the stars on them, that looked like broken-off dagger tips. We saw them destroying the secret airport that was nearby. The women screamed as the wings of our waiting planes caught fire and were sent hurtling through the air. We stood still in our tracks, stricken, unable to find the words to speak.

My father thought that the officer's visit had something to do with donations toward the war effort, so we seated him in the diwan and gave him our warmest welcome. But as he sat there in silence, we grew anxious. The officer, too, was uneasy. After drinking a cup of tea, he had fixed his gaze on the two rifles hanging from the wall. Noticing this, my father observed in passing, "They're licensed. We're at the foot of the mountain here, as you know, and besides, we have to protect our farmlands."

The officer replied, as if defending himself against an accusation, "I know that, ya hagg. God forbid we should be suspicious of you. You're a blessing on us all." But having said these words, he lapsed again into silence, and we into our fears. For it was rare that a visit by a government official was anything but bad news.

After a prolonged silence, the officer managed to find the words to tell my father what it was he wanted. He cleared his throat and shifted his position in his chair. Then he said, "You're aware, ya hagg, that the outlaws have been coming here."

Laughing and raising his hands in the air, my father replied, "God forbid, my friend, that I should be the one who invited them. If the government wants to see to the matter, I won't interfere."

The officer seemed confused. "See to the matter how, ya hagg?" he said.

My father answered, "I mean, if you want to arrest them when they come . . ."

I understood that my father had only said this in order to clear himself of any official blame. For he, like the miqaddis Bishai, did not believe in handing over one's guests, and he knew the truth of the matter as well as the officer, who exclaimed in surprise, "Did I say we were going to arrest them, ya hagg? How? You know they have machine guns and automatic rifles, and that there are more weapons to every two or three of them than we have in all of headquarters."

My father sighed and shook his head. "Well," he said, "in that case, what is there that I can do, sir? If that's where the government stands, then what on earth can I do?"

The officer replied, "Don't do anything . . ."

Then he glanced uneasily at me. "Could we speak privately?" he said to my father.

I stood up of my own accord.

The business didn't take long. I saw my father's expression

relax as he was seeing the officer to the outskirts of the village, where his car was waiting for him. I noticed a slight smile on his lips from where I stood waiting for him by the diwan, and as he approached me, he burst out laughing, unable to contain himself. He put his hand on my shoulder and said, "By God, your father's become a diplomat!"

He said no more than this, but I was to know everything when the outlaws came for their first visit after that event. We were sitting, as usual, on the sand outside the monastery walls: Harbi, Faris with some of his men, my father, and I; the miqaddis Bishai was not with us on that afternoon. The outlaws had eaten and drunk tea, but the kettle still sat on the open fire, which crackled away, occasionally throwing out a series of sparks. And for a little while that was the only sound to be heard.

The sun began to set, and two or three stars appeared in the sky. The outlaws, as was their wont, were about to begin getting ready to go, so they could catch the eight-o'clock train. Harbi looked tired, and it didn't appear that the visit would be prolonged, or that it would be a night for singing.

My father broke the silence, saying casually, "Tell me, ya miʿallim Faris . . . do you all come to Luxor by train or by car?"

Faris looked at my father in some surprise. "Ya hagg," he said, "you know . . . if we could get hold of cars, we'd drive, but there aren't always cars to be found." Then he laughed, adding, "As you see, there's quite a large number of us—*bismillaahi maa shaaʾ allah*—so we generally take the train."

Without looking at Faris, my father said in the same tone, "That is to say, it's hard to arrange transportation by car, ya miʿallim?"

Faris replied, "We can't arrange it every time."

"There's something behind your question, son of my father," said Harbi. "What's on your mind?" Waving his hand with an air of nonchalance, my father answered him, "Nothing, really . . . that is, it's the authorities. You realize the state of things in this country these days, after the war. I mean, if you didn't pass all together, as a group, through the streets of Luxor for the time being, it might be better that way."

The miʿallim Faris understood. He placed both hands on his head, and said, "By my eye and my head, ya hagg. You're the boss. For your sake and for Harbi's sake, we'll do whatever headquarters wants."

But Hinein objected. "How can you say that, ya miʿallim?" he demanded. "Tomorrow they'll ask us to turn ourselves in! What business is it of theirs if we ride the train, or . . ." My father interrupted him in some agitation, "What's the meaning of this talk, Hinein?" he said. "The authorities know why you come here, and they know that you observe the rules when you come and when you return peaceably. Have they given you any trouble before now? This is a request, for my sake and for Harbi's sake."

But Hinein went on as before, saying, "But what business is it of the authorities', ya hagg, if we . . ."

"Shut up, Hinein!" shouted Faris. Then he turned to my father. Lowering his voice, he said, "As I told you, ya hagg, you have only to ask." Then Faris began to rub his chin, looking thoughtful. He leaned his upper body toward my father and said, "By God, you've got me thinking, ya hagg. My blood's been boiling ever since the day those bastards took Sinai. Tell the commissioner that the miʿallim Faris is ready to take his men to Sinai to fight those Jews until they leave the country."

"What are you saying, ya miʿallim?" my father said, bewildered.

Faris replied seriously, "Tell our esteemed commissioner that the miʿallim Faris says to you that he and his men, the outlaws of all Upper Egypt, are ready to go to Sinai to drive out the Jews. We wouldn't be men if we stayed here while those bastards are there."

My father kept silent, and Harbi said sadly, "If only I still had the strength to speak the way you do, ya miʿallim."

"What kind of talk is this?" Faris replied hotly. "Tomorrow you'll be as strong as a horse, my friend—this sickness will pass, God willing."

But Harbi shook his head without conviction, and again there was silence.

My father leaned toward me and pulled me closer to him. Whispering in my ear and struggling not to laugh, he said, "Didn't I tell you? Your father's become a diplomat!"

Then he sighed, and said in a louder voice, "Well, it's getting late . . ."

Hinein had stood up and begun pacing in circles around the miʿallim Faris. Then in a sudden burst of enthusiasm he exclaimed, "By God, that's a great idea, man! But we'll need weapons."

Faris replied calmly, "The hagg will speak to the commissioner, and the army will give us weapons."

"Fair enough," said Hinein, "but that will take time."

He was quiet for a few moments. Then he said, as if he had

just remembered something, "By the way, ya miʿallim, I've heard that this monastery is full of gold."

But before the words were even out of his mouth, and before we realized anything was up, a shot had rung out. Hinein was sprawled on the ground, screaming, while the miʿallim Faris stood waving a pistol and shouting, "My name is Faris! I am Faris, you dog! And Faris does not betray his friends, you traitor!" Everyone had gotten to his feet. Harbi was clutching Faris's hand that held the pistol. Trying to calm his friend, he said in a voice that broke as he struggled for breath, "Enough, Faris . . . you've punished him, now, that's enough." Hinein lay sprawled on his stomach with his arms wrapped around his head, crying out in terror, "Please, ya miʿallim . . . I was joking . . . it's enough you've wrecked my leg!"

Neither Harbi nor my father succeeded in wresting the pistol from Faris's hand, but they were able to persuade him to sit down. He spoke in a voice that filled the mountain, saying, "This dog will get out of my sight . . . He will not stay with me one minute after this day."

"Whatever you say, ya miʿallim," said Harbi soothingly, "just calm down."

Once he felt safe enough, Hinein sat up. Moaning, he said, "You'd throw me out because of a joke, ya miʿallim?" Hardly able to control himself, Faris replied in a pained voice, "Do you want me, Hinein, to turn on these monks, whose protection, according to the Qur'an, is enjoined by our Lord—may he be praised and exalted?"

Turning then to my father for confirmation, he said, "Isn't that so, ya hagg?"

"The monks are mentioned in the Holy Qur'an, ya mi'allim," my father replied cautiously.

"Did you hear that?" said Faris to Hinein. "Are you testing me, Hinein, or are you a traitor to your own people? Who are you to reckon with Faris, ya Hinein?"

In a voice once again filled with pain, he repeated, more quietly this time, "Who are you to reckon with Faris? If it hadn't been for Faris, at one time . . ." Then he fell silent, his head bowed. After a little while he said to my father, "When will you give me an answer?"

"Answer to what, ya mi'allim?" my father replied, confused.

But Faris had already turned away from my father and directed his attention to Hinein. In a voice just as calm as before, he said, "Go on, Hinein. Get out of here."

"Ya mi'allim," Hinein groaned, almost in tears, "I'm your servant, here at your side for life . . ."

But Faris shook his head. "If you sell your own people for gold today," he said, "tomorrow you'll sell me for a penny." After a moment he went on. "Go, Hinein," he said shortly. "You no longer have a living with me."

At that moment, we noticed that the miqaddis Bishai was hurrying toward us, and that some of the other monks had gathered at the gate and were staring at us in silence.

Bishai, who was carrying cotton and gauze, knelt beside Hinein, who was still sitting, clutching his knee. "Did the bullet enter the bone?" he asked.

Then, examining the wounded man's leg, he went on, "I knew it hadn't gone in that far, but it's a large wound all the same, Hinein. Let me clean it for you."

The miqaddis Bishai was speaking in a deep, quavery voice I

had never heard before. I couldn't see his face, but I thought he might very well be crying.

Hinein stretched out his leg, submitting to the treatment, as the miqaddis Bishai cleaned the wound caused by the bullet, which had struck him below the knee. Hinein moaned when the tincture of iodine stung the wound. Bishai kept drying the blood and cleaning out the wound, laughing briefly, intermittently, a laugh that was nothing like his usual clear, loud laughter. "I told you," he said to the injured man, "leave this path. You didn't take my advice, and now look where it's gotten you."

Hinein shouted at Bishai to be quiet and do his job, and let ill enough alone.

But Bishai, after he finished bandaging Hinein's leg, patted him and, repeating that strange laugh, said, "Do you know your own religion, Hinein?" Rubbing his leg, Hinein replied sarcastically, "Why don't you teach me, ya miqaddis?" As if he hadn't heard, the miqaddis continued, "Did you know, Hinein, that our Savior washed Judas's feet on the night of the last supper?"

"I'd forgotten that," answered Hinein, in a mixture of pain and mockery, "so I thank the Lord you've reminded me."

Bishai rose to his feet and looked at the sky, crying out in a loud voice, as if in protest against all the world's injustices. Then he said, "But afterward Judas betrayed, ya Hinein. He betrayed."

CHAPTER FOUR

Al-naksa

Our police commissioner, Assayyed Hamza, was unusual for a policeman. He was of a very wealthy family from our village's governorate. Most of the time, he was busier looking after his properties than he was with his job as a police officer. As a result, no one was very much concerned about him, one way or the other. He changed dramatically, however, after we lost Sinai to Israel. He took to staying at work all day and night. In a corner of his office, he set up a camp bed, which could be folded up during the day and leaned against the wall in the corner. Besides this, he stopped wearing his jacket with the eagle and stars on it and began wearing only a khaki shirt with the sleeves rolled up above the elbow. He took to making the rounds of the town, to help keep the peace and to collect donations toward the war effort. He invited the heads of the feuding families to his office to negotiate reconciliations among them and get them to make a truce in his presence, placing their hands on copies of the Qur'an. In this way, they would renounce all their disputes. One of the things he did during this period was to send one of his officers to deliver to my father the message that recommended the disappearance of the band of outlaws from the streets of the town, in an effort to maintain the prestige of the security forces in these difficult times.

But the most important project he undertook in the days following Egypt's defeat in Sinai was military training. He opened up all the police headquarters to volunteers, and the able-bodied men in the town and the surrounding villages came out in droves to volunteer. The commissioner began to supervise all their training on his own, in small groups. And in those days I was, like the other high school students, among the crowd of volunteers. Early in the morning we would go to the police department. We would find Assayyed Hamza standing there in his military stance, ready to line us up in rows and whip us into shape. He gave hell to anyone who strayed from his row or whose posture was sloppy or slouching. Once he had given us his directions, he would instruct one of the officers or sergeants major to take us through Luxor in a "demonstration procession." So we would march in military step, stamping our feet and chanting loudly, "God is great, God is great," and "Egypt, Egypt, Mother Egypt," and "Arabs under one flag forever!" and so on, until our voices grew hoarse and we raised clouds of dust in all the city streets. Thus Luxor was ablaze with enthusiasm, ready for liberation, just as in ancient times. The commissioner, in a spirit of optimism, dubbed us the "Brigade of Amosis"—after Amosis, who had driven out the Hyksos. But just when we got to the next step—that is, when Assayyed Hamza stood before our orderly lines of boys, all standing at attention, and began to take apart a Kalashnikov rifle and to explain all its parts to us, in preparation for rifle training—instructions came south from Cairo that he was to take things easy and not to push so hard. And sure enough, when one day we went for our training session, we found a large sign in front of the police department, on which was an announcement in big letters that training was postponed until further notice and that the volunteers would be contacted at the appropriate time.

But that time never did come.

My father mediated between the miʿallim Faris and our respected commissioner Assayyed Hamza during the period that followed the discontinuance of military training activities. He had gone back to wearing his jacket, and the camp bed had disappeared from his office. After my father had drunk the coffee that the commissioner ordered for him and said what he had to say, Assayyed Hamza clapped his palms together and said, "This is all we need. Don't we have enough problems?"

"Why do you say that?" my father asked. "This is our chance to rid all Upper Egypt of the outlaws."

The commissioner shook his head. "Others will appear in their place, ya hagg," he said. "You know that. And outlaws we know are better than ones we don't."

My father sighed. "Believe me, ya bey," he said, "these days people are fed up with everything, including crime. Look, here's Faris, who's found our province hopping from one foot to the other with anxiety. He's ready to leave everything and go fight the Jews. Let him go! Speak to the people in government—maybe they can get some use out of him. If there's one thing the outlaws are good at, damn them, it's killing. If they don't succeed in driving out the Jews entirely, they'll at least give them a run for their money."

The commissioner stood up. "I'm afraid that's impossible, ya hagg," he said. "You want people to say I'm crazy?"

"God forbid, sir," my father replied. "The man wants to go, and with him the rest of the outlaws. What's wrong with that?"

"A lot, ya hagg," answered Assayyed Hamza. "Use your head." The commissioner was pointing his index finger at his own head. "Suppose they actually did drive out the Jews, and then they decided to stay put in Sinai? How would we get them out of there?"

My father had no answer to this. He bowed his head, trying not to smile.

Then Assayyed Hamza snapped to attention, pointed at my father, and said to him as if issuing a military order, "Listen, ya hagg. Tell Faris that what he can do right now to help the war effort is give up his criminal activity in the province."

But my father had a clear answer this time. He raised his head, looked Assayyed Hamza straight in the eye, and said calmly, "I can't tell him that, sir."

The commissioner said nothing for a moment. He seemed to be at a loss. Then he concluded the discussion. "Put him off then," he said. "Tell him the government will consider his offer."

My father had to wait until Faris's next visit to put him off.

The leader of the outlaws was sitting next to my father on the sand, his chin cupped in his hand, his eyes lidded. When he had heard the commissioner's message, he looked up. Laughing shortly, he said, "Well, if the government doesn't want us, then let everyone look out for himself."

After that, he stayed away for a long time.

But we had other things to worry about. For Harbi's health

had begun to decline rapidly. My father kept replenishing the many medications that had been prescribed for Harbi by the doctors in Cairo, and we kept bringing them to him, but he only got thinner and thinner. He also became more withdrawn and silent. Food disgusted him, especially meat, which he would not touch, although the miqaddis Bishai and I, if we were all eating together, would keep pressing him to eat something. One time, as he was lying in front of his hut, his head resting on his arm, his gaze wandering, I asked him, "What's wrong with you, Harbi? What is this sickness of yours?"

In a barely audible voice he replied, "I'm like a sterile palm tree, my young friend, that gives no dates and casts no shade. I was finished a long time ago, but death won't have me."

The miqaddis Bishai was standing near us. Forcing a laugh, he said, "A palm tree can't be sterile, Harbi, unless its roots are too lazy to drink. So why are you lazy? Eat and drink, and you'll thrive and cover a feddan with your shade!"

Harbi answered, "And if the roots are dead, ya migaddis?"

Leaning on his hoe, Bishai turned his face away from us, saying, "The roots don't die except by the will of our Lord, my son. So why are you killing them off yourself? Why do you kill them with your own hand?"

Harbi's gaze also wandered into the distance, and he said nothing.

Aunt Safiyya was even more upset about Harbi's health than my father, the miqaddis Bishai, or I. She had been heard to wish him recovery and long life. She asked all his visitors how he was doing, suggesting that they should tell my father to bring doctors from Asyut, or better yet, from Cairo if possible. It was said that at one of the wakes she burst into tears and began striking her cheeks. "It will be the ruin of me," she cried, "if Harbi should die. Alas for me, and for you, ya Hassaan, if Harbi dies! What will I say to the bey? Tell me, all of you, what will I say to the bey? 'We let him die before taking our revenge and putting out the fire of your torment!'"

It was said that she wouldn't calm down or stop strewing her face and hair with dust until one of the women swore to her that her husband had visited Harbi at the monastery a few days before and seen how the color had flooded back into his face, and how he was once more as strong as a horse.

If only that had been the truth; in reality, Harbi was getting worse day by day. The treatments of the doctors from Asyut and the capital didn't do any good, and neither did the herbal cures of the miqaddis Bishai, who now attended Harbi constantly and was almost never away from his hut.

But we were distracted even from this, when we were struck by yet a new calamity, such as we had never known before. For the first time, highway robbers turned up in the hills about the village. It started with some shepherds who ran into trouble. These boys, with their sheep and goats, roamed the area that lay in the direction of the mountain, in search of grass. One day they came back and reported that they had been beaten up, their heads bashed and their sheep stolen. They cried as they told how a gang had descended on them from behind the mountain. The gang had first shot their dogs, then driven the boys off, beating and battering them with the butts of their rifles.

After that, these criminals started showing up on the road leading to Luxor, where they attacked and robbed travelers by night. It was said that their leader, who always rode a black horse, was a man who knew no mercy. He would strip whomever he met of everything he had. As for those who had no money—if they had the bad luck to fall into his hands, he would make an example of them, stripping them of their clothes and then showering them with blows, insults, and curses for "pretending to be human beings, coming and going on the roads as if they were sons of the consul." He would swear that if he ever saw one of them again, he would kill him.

So after sunset, the road to Luxor became a no-man's-land for everyone, whether he owned anything or not. The farmers began to go out in groups to guard the crops. They would gather in a field in the midst of their farms, to watch over all the land. This didn't prevent the theft of some of the harvest. The head watchman, along with the rest of his men, blocked all approaches to the village throughout the night. But in spite of all these activities, as well as the efforts of the police force, they did not manage to lay hands on either the robbers or their leader.

Everyone assumed these men had taken refuge in the mountain caves, well out of reach.

During those black days, Harbi's visitors came less often. At that time, I was in the final year of high school and was preoccupied with trying to get good grades, but this was not the reason I saw less of Harbi. It was just that a journey onto the mountain, all the way to the monastery, was no longer a simple matter. I had always used to make this trip on foot, sometimes twice a day—and others did the same. Now, however, no one made the trip to visit Harbi unless he was with a group. And we went armed with rifles.

Unfortunately, Faris and his men also stopped visiting Harbi during this period. In fact, a rumor went around that those thieves who were causing all the trouble were none other than the outlaws themselves. Some said that the village had begun to look good to the outlaws, after they had spent time there and gotten to know the place. Those with more sense responded, "So what makes them leave the wealthy areas in the north of the province and pay so much attention to our poor village?"

This was not the only explanation suggested for the trouble. There were also those who said that all these things plagued our village because it had been defiled by drunkenness. The fact was, more customers started frequenting the secret room at the back of Rizq's grocery during that time, in order to drink ʿaraq. So when it seemed that there would be no end to the village's troubles, the mayor, as a precautionary measure, decided to put an end to the "defilement" by forcing Rizq to stop serving ʿaraq. It was said that the mayor even made him pour out all the ʿaraq he had stored away. Then the merrymakers had to confine their nightly entertainments to smoking the gouza—which was kept filled with a never-ending supply of hashish—and listening to the radio. On those nights, they would tell jokes that were repeated next day around the village. They said, for instance, that the bandits had found the mayor Hamid Asran returning from Luxor one night, but when they frisked him, they found him so broke that they took pity on him, gave him a few pennies, and sent him on his way. They joked that the mayor had made a complaint to the United Nations, which had denounced the bandits, declaring that their papers had been sent north to Cairo . . . and that sort of thing.

Sometimes I would pass these jokes on to my father, who listened in silence, without smiling. But his silence goaded me on, and I kept repeating to him the things I had heard, until one day he flared up in my face, shouting, "Don't you have studying to do? If you can't do any good in this calamity, then stick to your lessons and shut up!" My father had never once told me off, since the time he came to consider me a man—but that day he did.

Another thing that happened around that time was that old Brother Metri, the head of the monastery, died—may he rest in peace. The monk who replaced him was not one of those at that monastery but had been sent from the north. The miqaddis Bishai continued to run his usual weekly errands in Luxor, but the new head insisted that other monks accompany him and help carry the purchases, and that they return from Luxor before noon. When we would visit Harbi, the miqaddis Bishai would greet us with his irrepressible laughter and tell us not to worry or upset ourselves about the bandits. He said that this was a plague sent down upon our country and that it would come to an end. "The Lord sent plagues to our country before, seven different times, and then the people's affliction was lifted," he said. "This too will come to an end, by God's will." We would ask him anxiously, "But when, ya miqaddis Bishai?"

"Soon," he would reply, "God willing."

Everyone now hoped that the miqaddis Bishai really was in contact with the spirits and that the spirits had told him the truth this time.

Even now, after all these years, it still amazes me that we did not figure out right at the start what the miqaddis Bishai had realized, by his simple and perceptive intuition.

On that wintry morning, it was said, he was working the land, pulling weeds from among the crops. Harbi was sitting near him, crouched in the sun, seeking its warmth. They said that the miqaddis Bishai suddenly stopped what he was doing, stood up straight, then turned to face Harbi. He stood scratching his forehead. Then he said, "Ya Harbi . . . in the beginning . . . I mean, son, in the very beginning . . . did the Evil One choose Woman, or did Woman choose the Evil One?"

Harbi was used to the miqaddis Bishai's way of speaking and his strange questions. Smiling, he said, "Ya migaddis, look at me —cast down here in this place with you, and you ask me questions about women? What do I know about women, when I'm here all the time? Let me out of the monastery, and I'll give you an answer."

Bishai laughed. "No, ya Harbi," he said, "you'll give me an answer before nightfall!"

Harbi said later that he hadn't understood why Bishai kept glancing in the direction of the mountain every few seconds.

But could the miqaddis Bishai's hearing have been that sharp?

Harbi said that Bishai suddenly left him and ran toward the mountain, spreading his arms as wide as he could, as if to stop the black horse and its masked rider, who had appeared from behind a rock. He said Bishai was shouting in a voice that echoed off the mountain,

"Get away, ya Hinein! Get away, ya Judas, God's curse on you!"

It was that cry, said Harbi, that saved his life, for the bullet struck right next to him where he squatted on the ground. He said that the rifle shook in Hinein's hand at that moment and that the horse reared up on its hind legs, so that Harbi was able to take out a pistol from his pocket and aim it at Hinein's heart as he shot. Hinein twisted on his horse, crumpling in the saddle, and galloped off onto the mountain. At that moment, Bishai was weeping and running toward the mountain, shouting, "Ya Hinein, come back! Why did you wander away from the fold, why did you forsake our Lord? Come back, ya Hinein! The stray lamb may also enter the Kingdom of Heaven, if he comes back to the fold . . . so come back!"

But Hinein was far away by that time.

That evening a starving horse turned up in the village. It wandered with its head down, taking what food it could get from the earth and trailing a ribbon of blood behind it. When they took Hinein down from its back, they found he had given up the ghost.

We were told that when the news reached my aunt Safiyya, she began to sob, "Witness, ya bey, that I tried! Even with the outlaws, I tried! And I swear I'll keep trying until you can sleep peacefully in your grave! Harbi will never get the better of us!"

In the morning, Father Maximus, head of the monastery, sent Brother Girgis to request a meeting with my father. He and I went together.

It was the first time I had seen Father Maximus. I found him to be rather short, and even-tempered, with small eyes that glittered with intelligence. He shook hands with my father. He shook hands with me, too, and asked how my schoolwork was going. Then he turned back to my father and said with a slight smile, "Since I arrived at this monastery, ya hagg, I've heard more singing and shooting than praying. This is a circus."

My father replied anxiously that this would not happen again, God willing.

The leader of the monastery frowned slightly. "I believe," he said, "that when Brother Metri, God rest his soul, agreed to give sanctuary to Harbi, he set a reasonable condition. He asked that no weapons enter the monastery, since the houses of worship, and even the monastery's farmlands, are no place for playing with guns. Now, what am I to say to the police and the investigator, when they come to the monastery and start giving us the third degree?"

My father told Father Maximus to rest easy on this point, for there would be no police and no investigation.

Our mayor, Hamid Asran, had made sure of that in his own way, the day before. For when people found out about what had happened and the news began to spread, from the monastery and from Safiyya's house, the village men gathered in front of the mayor's house, where they began arguing loudly and making an uproar. Some said that it was Hinein who had offered his services to Safiyya as Harbi's assassin. They said he had demanded thousands of pounds in hard cash and that she hadn't quibbled with him about the price. Others said it was the other way around: that it was Safiyya who had set Hinein and his men on our village, after Faris had sent him away. They began pointing out that most of the people who had been beaten up or had their crops stolen were among Harbi's close friends and visitors.

But then the mayor Hamid came out shouting at the crowd. "Not a word, you lowlifes!" he said. "The head watchman set up this thief and arranged his death. Anyone who says otherwise—I'll cut his tongue out! And whoever brings up the subject of Harbi or anyone else will have me to answer to!"

Was there anyone who wanted anything different from what the mayor wanted: for the village to have done with that whole business, once and for all?

Father Maximus seemed somewhat relieved when he heard what had happened. All the same, he demanded that my father see to it that Harbi turn over his pistol and that no more weapons find their way into the monastery.

When he got up to see us off, at the monastery door he said to my father, "By the way, ya hagg—I don't believe that hut is a suitable place for your cousin to stay. If a room could be built for him, or a small house, near the mountain, he'd still be under the protection of the monastery, wouldn't he?

My father understood. He promised the head of the monastery that he would do his best. But he was grief stricken, and spoke not a word to me on the way home.

But there was no need for all this.

Only a few days had passed, and my father had not yet begun building a new place for Harbi, when we were startled one morning by a voice crying out in the distance, then coming nearer to our house. Hurrying outside in alarm, we saw the miqaddis Bishai running toward us without his belt tied around his waist, his clothes and indeed his whole person in disarray. Alternately weeping and gasping for breath, he said, "Hurry, ya hagg! Hurry! The Lord is calling his lamb back to the fold . . ."

My father burst out crying as well and began running toward the monastery just as he was, in his indoor clothes. I ran right behind him. He didn't think of waiting a moment until we could saddle a mount. It didn't occur to us for an instant that this could save us any time. This was the only time in my life I ever saw my father weep. "My God," he cried incoherently, "have mercy . . . my God! Are you satisfied now Safiyya? I won't get to see Harbi before he dies, ya Safiyya! My God! I want to see him—please God!"

And God answered my father's prayer. When we got to the monastery, Harbi was lying there, his gaze wandering vaguely, his breath barely lifting his chest. But he was able to recognize us. My father drew his head onto his lap so that it was pointing in the direction of Mecca, and Harbi reached out to take his hand. He spoke, his voice coming very faintly. "Forgive me," he said, "son of . . . my . . . my father . . ."

But my father said, "No, it's you who must forgive us, ya Harbi! My brother . . . my son . . . oh dear God . . . !"

My father helped him say the creed, "There is no god but God, and Muhammad is His prophet." Then my father closed Harbi's eyes. He leaned over, clasping him in his arms, and wept.

At the door to the hut, the miqaddis Bishai was standing and staring, wide-eyed, unable at that moment to weep. When he saw me crying, he took me strongly in his arms, then held me away from him a little, one hand still on my shoulder. His other hand trembled as he gestured with it toward the body stretched out on the ground, while his eyes grew still wider. He said to me in amazement, "Look, son . . . look. He, too, lived to suffer. Do you see?"

Only then did he find his tears. His sobs answered my own and those of my father, who was still hunched over the dead body.

Epilogue

Harbi's funeral passed by the palace, which had not been opened once since Aunt Safiyya left it. I happened to glance toward its gate, which was coated with rust. I saw the European palm trees with their dried-up leaves hanging there, a dull brown color. I shivered as I walked in the sad procession, repeating the incantation, "There is no god but God, there is no god but God."

My aunt Safiyya did not last long after Harbi's passing.

It was said that she was standing in the courtyard of her house, with Hassaan beside her, when the news was brought to her. She snatched up Hassaan from the ground with a great shriek and flung him at the wall with all her strength. Had one of the servant women not caught him, his head would have been smashed.

It was said that afterward she sat down on the ground and whispered, "He died by God's hand? He died by God's hand? Do you see, ya bey? Why have you done this to me?" Then she cried out for the last time, "Why have you done this to me, all of you, God's curse upon you all!"

It was said that she then got up and went into her room. After that she spoke not a word, tasting neither food nor drink.

They told my father what had happened, and he brought her a doctor from Luxor. She was nearly in a coma when he examined her. He prescribed intravenous feeding for her. But in spite of that, she continued to slip rapidly away.

They said that whenever she would regain consciousness for a little while, she would pull the needles from her arms. She refused to be taken to the hospital, and the doctor said there was nothing to be done.

I would go with my father to visit her during those days, but by that time she was unable to recognize anyone. One day, though, she came out of her coma and looked at my father, who was sitting by her bedside. She stared at him awhile with weary eyes that had not lost their beauty, in spite of how much she had wasted away. In a faint voice she said, "Yes, father. Excuse me, I can't get up. But if Harbi asks for my hand, tell the bey I agree. You must speak for me, father . . . and I agree to any dowry Harbi proposes . . . don't worry about the dowry . . ."

She closed her eyes again, and it was then that she went into her final coma.

I was back in the village for summer vacation, after passing my second-year exams in the school of archaeology, when I witnessed the conclusion of those events.

The village was changing, and so was the monastery. New monks came, educated ones, and a big library was installed in the hall of "Kabb el-Noor," which had been refurbished and given a fresh coat of paint. I went occasionally to that library to study, but for the first time I began to feel self-conscious and embarrassed, because I no longer knew any of the monks really well, other than Brother Girgis, and the library was not his domain. The new monks were polite and always ready to help me in my research, but few of them spoke our Saʿiidi dialect or knew the history of our village.

The miqaddis Bishai no longer went to Luxor to buy supplies for the monastery. Now he was always on the farm.

Sometimes he worked at training the new monks in farming, but most of the time he sat in his hut, singing his sad hymns to the Virgin Mary. From time to time, he would come to the village, his beard untrimmed and his clothing unkempt, and he seemed to be aging rapidly. He passed through the fields as usual, giving advice to the farmers as was his custom, but he would always ask about Harbi. He would ask whether anyone had seen him. He would say that he was very concerned, because Harbi had left his hut, and he was afraid someone might harm him. He said that Hinein was laying a trap for him and was planning to turn him in to the police, because Hinein had accepted some pieces of silver.* Bishai told the farmers that if they saw Harbi, they should bring him back to the monastery.

Then one morning, Brother Girgis came looking for my father. He said that the head of the monastery wanted his help. He said they needed a carriage to take the miqaddis Bishai to the hospital, as no taxi driver was willing to risk driving

*This is a reference to Judas's betrayal of Christ, in exchange for thirty pieces of silver.

on the rough dirt road to the monastery, so could my father please help?

My father was alarmed. "What's wrong with Bishai?" he asked. "Why are you taking him to the hospital?"

Brother Girgis leaned toward my father, taking him by the shoulder, and whispered something in his ear. My father was taken aback. "But why?" he said. "What's new about that? All his life the miqaddis Bishai has been this way. The whole village knows him and is used to him. He's never hurt anyone in his life, so what's the reason for this?" Brother Girgis once again leaned toward my father and whispered in his ear. My father bowed his head sadly. Then he sighed, and told Brother Girgis to go back to the monastery and that he would work something out.

I understood without asking, and sadly followed my father so that we could hook up the horse and carriage one last time. We had decided to stop using it when cars began to appear more and more frequently on the airport road, and it got to be faster and easier to use them. It seemed to me that our skinny old horse had a surprised look in his eye as he watched us harnessing him to the carriage, with its rusty wheels.

I tried to get up into the front seat to drive the carriage, but my father held his hand out in front of my face and said firmly, "No. You stay here."

In mild protest, I answered my father, "But you know that I love the miqaddis Bishai."

Putting his hand on my shoulder, he replied, "That's why I want you to stay behind. Let me go alone. Believe me, even I don't want to go, this time."

My father's mind was made up. I stayed behind. I stood there, following him with my eyes as he headed east in the carriage toward the monastery, ever so slowly.

Although Brother Girgis had spoken with no one but my father, it was impossible to keep any news secret in our village. Within a short time, I was standing with a group of villagers, who gathered in a row at the point where the road turned to dirt, not far from our house. We stood watching the carriage as it approached from afar, swaying, while my father cracked the whip, and yanked on the reins, then let them out, trying to get the horse moving, for it had forgotten how to run. But my father's efforts were all in vain. The horse plodded along, barely even at a walk, and he stumbled as if he were about to fall at any moment.

Silence fell on the men standing there, when the carriage reached us. We could see the miqaddis Bishai clearly . . . and yet it wasn't Bishai. For some reason, they had taken away his black robe and dressed him in an ordinary gallabiyya. They had shaved his head and his face, so that his face looked extremely small and strange, with two circles of startling white where his hair and beard had been.

Brother Girgis was on his right and another monk, whom I didn't know, was on his left, the two of them holding him by the arms. Everyone fell silent as the carriage passed sluggishly before our eyes. But then one of the farmers who were standing there made a sudden movement. He was holding a stick or a hoe—I don't remember which—and this he held up and waved, saying in a voice that trembled, "Goodbye, ya Bishai . . . God be with you, ya Bishai!"

Bishai looked at us with his wide-open eyes, recognized me,

and managed to free his right arm from Brother Girgis's grasp. He waved at me, smiling, and said, "Give my greetings to . . ."

Although I was unable to hear the name of whoever it was he wanted me to greet for him, I guessed who it might be. I ran behind the carriage, calling in my turn, "Goodbye, ya migaddis . . . God be with you . . ."

As if the horse had been alarmed by all this shouting, he began to trot for the first time, rocking my father in his seat. Then the carriage disappeared from sight amidst the alleyways of the village.

How many years have gone by?

Here I am now, living in Cairo with my mother, who moved in with me after the death of my father. Once my sisters had married and I had graduated, my father fulfilled his pledge to make the pilgrimage to Mecca twice: once for himself and once for Harbi. And it fell out as he had wished, for he died while on the second pilgrimage and was buried in Medina, near his beloved Prophet, blessings and peace be upon him.

As for my sisters, not one of them lives in the village anymore. They all married relatives of ours who were university graduates. Ward es-Sham lives with her husband in Saudi Arabia, while Sikeena has emigrated to Canada and Ruqayya lives in Alexandria. Abla did not marry Hassaan, who is younger than she is; rather she works with her husband for a branch of an import-export company, owned by Hassaan, in Germany.

She and the rest of my sisters, with their children, come for visits to Cairo, but we rarely gather together all at the same time. My mother sometimes weeps over her loneliness, asking what can have happened.

As for me, I still work in archaeology, and I seldom go back to the village.

I know that there is electricity now in all the village houses and that no one uses lanterns anymore. I know that the road to the monastery has been paved and that many tourists now go to see the relics, just as the miqaddis Bishai used to wish.

One of my cousins is forever sending me reproachful letters, asking me why we closed up the house, leaving it empty and abandoned. He says that the walls are crumbling and the foundations cracking, and that there's no longer any use in renovating, but the house will have to be rebuilt entirely.

"Anyone without a house," he tells me, "tries to build one, so how can you let your house fall to ruin?" He keeps urging me to rebuild the house.

When I receive one of these letters, all my memories come flooding back to me, and I see everything just as it was a quarter of a century ago.

And I ask myself, is there still a child who brings cookies to the monastery in a white cardboard box?

And I ask myself, do the monks still give their neighbors those small-pitted, sugared dates?

I ask myself . . .

Time and again, I ask myself . . .